TEMPTATION

Also available from Headline Liaison

Seduction by Cathryn Cooper
Change Partners by Cathryn Cooper
Obsession by Cathryn Cooper
Green Silk by Cathryn Cooper
Act of Exposure by Cathryn Cooper
The Journal by James Allen
Love Letters by James Allen
The Diary by James Allen
Out of Control by Rebecca Ambrose
Aphrodisia by Rebecca Ambrose
A Private Affair by Carol Anderson
Voluptuous Voyage by Lacey Carlyle
Magnolia Moon by Lacey Carlyle
Vermilion Gates by Lucinda Chester
The Challenge by Lucinda Chester
The Paradise Garden by Aurelia Clifford
Hearts on Fire by Tom Crewe and Amber Wells
Sleepless Nights by Tom Crewe & Amber Wells
Dangerous Desires by J J Duke
Seven Days by J J Duke
A Scent of Danger by Sarah Hope-Walker
Private Lessons by Cheryl Mildenhall
Intimate Strangers by Cheryl Mildenhall
Dance of Desire by Cheryl Mildenhall

Temptation

Cathryn Cooper

First published in 1997
by HEADLINE BOOK PUBLISHING

A HEADLINE LIAISON paperback

10 9 8 7 6 5 4 3 2 1

ISBN 0 7472 5628 4

Typeset by Palimpsest Book Production Limited,
Polmont, Stirlingshire
Printed and bound in Great Britain by
Mackays of Chatham PLC, Chatham, Kent

HEADLINE BOOK PUBLISHING
A division of Hodder Headline PLC
338 Euston Road
London NW1 3BH

Temptation

Chapter 1

Sunlight glinted on the chromium trim as the sleek, black Lagonda swung into the verge and came to a halt at the side of the road.

Mariella's eyelids flickered in a resentful fashion. She had just woken from a dream she had not wanted to leave. Putting her resentment aside, she took a deep breath and gazed out across the sea which lay some distance below them.

She glanced at her companion. 'Are we nearly there, Peter?'

His reply came slowly, as if he needed to think carefully before informing her of his opinion. 'Yes, my darling Mariella. A few more miles along this dreary road and we arrive at St Asaph which will no doubt smell of fish and grubby peasants.'

Mariella looked at him again, her stomach muscles tightening as his profile, his high cheekbones, his dark features infiltrated and ignited her senses. Peter had been made in the image of Valentino, yet didn't know it. Valentino was the man of her fantasy world, a place where the sheik waited to whisk her away on his fiery steed.

'Fishermen,' Mariella corrected.

'Peasants,' muttered Count Peter Stavorsky.

Lips quivering into a smile, he reached for her and placed his hand on her thigh, his fingers clawing at the soft cotton of her dress until only her stocking lay between his hand and her flesh. 'Are you excited by the prospect of assisting me with my quest?'

Mariella narrowed her eyes, shivered deliciously and gasped as his hand travelled above her stocking and over the pink bows of her garter. His palm was warm on her thigh.

She turned and looked into his eyes, her smile slow, her voice alluring. 'You always excite me, Peter.'

Her strength seemed to wither away as she looked up at him. For a brief moment, she imagined his dark looks half hidden by an Arabic headdress, his eyes smouldering with threat and with passion. Like Valentino, she thought. My idol. My dream lover.

Peter's smile gave her the confidence to reach for him. His jaw tightened. The smile disappeared as her fingers traced the shiny scar running down his cheek. A hardness came to his eyes which were already as black as coal.

Mariella, more wary now, let her hand fall away.

Peter grabbed her wrist. His voice grated. 'This quest is very important to me, Mariella. I could have approached things in another way rather than use you to obtain the icon that belonged to my family.' He smiled laconically and gently tucked her hair behind her ears as if she were a wayward child. 'But I know how you love sexual adventure, and you also know how I adore you telling me of your liaisons.' He kissed her lips. 'You tell them like a story, or a dream from which you have just woken. I like that. It holds a touch of innocence.'

The hand that was on her thigh went a little higher, his fingers gently brushing against the crotch of her silky knickers.

A dreamy look replaced the one of wariness. Mariella's lips fell open. Her breath came shorter, sharper as details of a daydream she had been having mixed with the sensations his hand had created.

Her knees gently parted and she pulled her dress a little higher. Peter took his hand away.

'Peter!' Her voice was breathless, pleading.

'Later, my darling. Save yourself.'

Mariella glanced down at her clenched thighs, then just as quickly, glanced defiantly at Peter.

Swiftly, her hands dived between her legs. Her hips heaved towards them just three times. The thrills ignited by Peter's hand easily and quickly converted into a fast but fulfilling orgasm.

Sighing and breathless, she closed her eyes, hands lying limply in her lap, breasts heaving as her body began to relax against the grey leather seat.

Even as Peter spoke, she kept her eyes closed, fearing to look at him.

'You are becoming defiant, Mariella,' he growled. 'What is happening to that young woman I first initiated into the art of love?'

Although Mariella felt his burning glare, she kept her eyes tightly closed and said nothing.

'You will learn,' he growled softly. 'You will learn.'

Once he had restarted the car, Mariella turned her face towards the window and stared out at the sea.

The breeze blew her hair across her face, and as it did so she wondered at the changes going on inside her. How much longer would she need Peter? How much longer would he need her?

As Peter lapsed into silence and the scenery sped by, Mariella drifted into one of her daydreams, a world where reality and fantasy mingled.

Beautiful as it was, she closed her eyes against the scenery and let herself slip slowly into a fantasy where she was submissive and her lover insatiable. He was always the same man.

To his fans he was simply Valentino. In Mariella's fantasy, he was simply 'The Sheik', but not nearly so tame a creature as she had seen in the darkness of the picture palace.

'You are my prisoner,' he told her, his dark eyes flashing as he threw her on to the red carpeted floor.

'Please,' she cried out, her breasts heaving beneath her neat, white blouse. 'Don't hurt me!'

His smile was cruel and a hint of menace came to his eyes. 'You are in no position to demand anything of me, woman. It is I who will demand everything of you. Now get to your feet.'

Slowly, eyes wide with apprehension, Mariella stood up.

Her breasts rose and fell as he loomed over her and she

looked up into his eyes. Her legs felt weak and the lips of her sex hung like lead weights between her legs.

His hands clasped her face tightly as his lips bruised her mouth, his tongue ramming inwards until it hit the back of her throat.

She tried to gag, tried to tear at his wrists to free herself. But he was stronger than her. Fuelled by anger as well as fear, she clenched her fists and pummelled at his biceps and shoulders. They were hard, and like the rest of his body, well formed, highly desirable.

He laughed when his mouth left hers, and she struggled. Still he held her tightly, laughing louder as she wriggled and wrenched her arms against his strength, his hands like iron bands around her wrists.

Then she kicked him.

His face darkened. Suddenly she showed fear although she felt only excitement. His expression thrilled her. It was as if that one kick had unjammed a very dangerous door.

Soon, his hands were on her shoulders, ripping at her clothes, his fingers raking her naked flesh. Her blouse, that had once been so white and neat, now lay in a crumpled, torn heap.

She attempted to reach for his face, to rake her nails down it, scar it till it ran with blood.

One fingernail succeeded in scouring his cheek. A thin trickle of blood appeared.

The sheik seemed to freeze, his eyes wide with anger. Mariella's whole body seemed to vibrate with excitement.

'You fight like a wild horse,' the desert leader exclaimed. 'And like a wild horse I will break you in. I will tame you so that I may ride and use you as I please.'

He called for his servants, two massive men wearing the white and black robes of the wandering Bedouin.

After he spoke to them in a language she did not understand, the rest of her clothes were taken from her body.

Automatically, she tried to cover herself with her hands,

but her wrists were held in a vice-like grip behind her back. A silken red rope with hanging gold tassels was wound around her wrists. A red leather collar decorated with gold studs was placed around her neck. From the collar hung a gold chain that was thick enough to be strong but not ugly.

Mariella tingled all over as the gold chain was looped into a metal ring half-way up the tent pole. The trailing end of the silk rope that held her hands was pulled tightly up to join the chain so that her arms were pulled well up towards her shoulder blades.

Her nipples rubbed against the harsh rope that was bound around the tent pole as she was pushed against it. Her belly felt its coarseness too, and her mons discovered a delicious sensation could be achieved simply by pressing more firmly against a large knot that was in the rope.

'Now we will start the breaking-in process,' hissed the sheik, his mouth just a breath from her ear. 'You will learn to obey me. Learn to submit to my every whim.'

Delectable shivers ran over her firm flesh as his palm ran down over her back before curving in turn over each of her buttocks.

'Such a beautiful body. Such beautiful orbs; like ripe pear halves, clinging to each other before dropping from the tree.' His voice was full of pent up passion that was fuelled by sheer lust.

She moaned as his finger traced the crack in between, its tip briefly dipping into the dark shadow between her legs.

'So much to explore,' he said huskily, and her legs went weak.

Chapter 2

The car swung from the headland and on to a road that wound down to the village below.

St Asaph, a small whitewashed town on the French Riviera, had slept through most of the centuries but was finally awakened with the dawning of the twentieth. Now, in 1927, it had been discovered by the rich, the sophisticated, and the merely decadent.

Hidden from the main thoroughfare that linked St Tropez, Villefranche, and other lesser known coastal settlements, it was reached by a track lined with fir trees which led off the main road and along a grassy green headland. At first sight the headland appeared to jut out into the glittering sea in the same way as a diving board does into a pool. But the track was deceitful. Three quarters of the way along its length, just at that point where it seemed there were only clouds and a blurred horizon up ahead, the track took a leftward swing and dived down a steep road to the village below.

Smart cars had replaced heavily-laden donkeys and trundling carts in a place where fishing had long been the main provider of daily bread.

Sweet young things, their dresses barely reaching their knees, their hair shingled into geometric bobs, far outnumbered the old women in dull black and sack aprons.

They giggled as they walked along the quay, their pert bottoms swinging in time with the twirling of ropes of beads that reached well below their navels. Their lips were plum or cherry red, their eyes dark with shadow, liner and mascara in blues, mauves and deep greens.

The sweet smell of lilac drifted on the air and the sun was getting warmer as noon approached.

Tall and slim, Mariella strolled along the quay where graceful yachts sat aloof from what remained of St Asaph's fishing fleet.

Mariella smiled with the certainty that she was walking provocatively, whilst looking sweetly innocent.

She was well aware that the swaying of her hips was having the right effect on the two men watching her. It was just a question of which one would be the first to be tempted. Both were handsome. Both were rich, and neither knew – nor were ever likely to admit – that she was baiting a hook for them as though they were fish. She was as flamboyantly attractive as a brightly coloured fly on a sharp, steel hook. Perhaps she was just as deadly. She had a quest to pursue, a task that excited her and promised adventures, according to her lover, Count Peter Stavorsky.

I don't need to do it, she told herself. If I wanted to, I could say no.

But the urge to embark on a real sexual adventure rather than an imagined one, was too great to ignore. The prospect thrilled her.

'You will do everything to tempt them,' Peter had whispered against her ear as they lay naked in her bed. 'Did you see their cars? Did you see their yachts? Can you imagine what they get up to in their villas? Can you imagine their naked bodies against yours?'

Closing her eyes, she had arched her back against his black-haired chest. The smell of him had filled her nostrils and made her tingle all over. A slow ache had throbbed in her loins as the insides of her thighs rubbed against the outside of his. The softness of his scrotum had teased against her sex, whilst the hardness of his cock had pressed almost painfully against her pubic bone.

'Yes. I will. I will!' she had cried, her voice seeming to crack in places as if she were in pain. 'Oh, I can imagine their bodies, the hair around their cocks, the hardness of their thighs.'

Pictures of naked, well-made men came to her mind, their

cocks hard, their bodies more beautiful in fantasy than reality could ever make them.

'Oh, yes,' she sighed again.

'And you will tempt them,' the count growled, his penis pulsating as it invaded her body. 'You are a temptation they will be unable to resist, and once in their confidence . . .' Through narrowed eyes, she saw a mocking smile play around his mouth as he held himself off from her. Only half of his erection was in her body.

'Oh, please,' Mariella moaned, her hips writhing, coercing him to bury himself to the hilt. 'Please . . .'

Covertly, she had watched his expression.

Peter's eyes had narrowed. His black brows suddenly meeting in a satanic vee. His jaw had become rigid. A few seconds later, sinews and muscles straining against his skin, he had thrust himself into her.

'You will complete your task!'

She had cried out, yelling for mercy, yet also yelling for more. Her body had moved to meet his assault.

A fine sweat had broken out over her body. She had wanted to cry 'enough', yet willed herself not to show him any weakness.

Just when she'd thought she could take no more, his tactics had altered. Fast turned to slow. She had sighed with pleasure as his lips had brushed against her throat, then found her nipples. In turn, her sigh had turned to a moan as he sucked long and lovingly.

Because her back had been arched, his hands had nimbly filled the gap then slid downwards to grasp her buttocks. Cries of protest did not stop him from digging his fingernails into her flesh.

'That hurts,' she had cried.

He had smiled that long, slow smile of his. His hair had fallen over his thick, dark brows. His sloping, black eyes were almost hidden by the silky curls.

He had shaken his head, his eyes unmerciful. 'It does not

hurt really, babushka. The truth is that you want it in you. You want to suck the life out of it with your body. Take my very essence. That is all you women ever want.' The tone of his voice had seemed to dwindle in the way of clockwork when it needs rewinding.

It had occured to her to protest that it was not so, but Mariella was a woman who knew what she wanted. Besides, just the rich tones of his voice made all the more exotic by his Russian accent, were enough to make her senses reel. She wanted to hear him speak again.

'I want my icon back,' he had said, withdrawing himself again so that only the tip of his penis had nudged at her entrance. 'Are you still willing to get it for me? Are you?'

She had mewed, wriggled, whined, and begged him to put his cock back into her, to impale her, to invade her, to fuck her. She had used all those words; let them tumble from her mouth in a demanding torrent along with a whole variety of expletives she had thought she would never use.

He had braced his arms, and she had held her legs wide apart. Opening her eyes, she had stared at the length and strength of his appendage. There it was, its tip still nuzzling against her vagina as he awaited her answer. His eyes held hers.

'Answer me. Are you willing to find out which man has my icon?'

Hungry for him to re-enter her body, Mariella had arched her back again, then raised her hips to meet his.

'Yes Peter,' she cried with wild abandon, flinging her head from side to side. 'Yes! Yes! Yes! Anything you want. Anything at all, but please, put it in me! Let me have it!'

Oh yes, she thought to herself as she walked seductively along the quay. Anything at all, Peter. You want your icon, I want adventures that, up until now, I have only dreamed of.

Chapter 3

Joseph Michael Carey III chewed on a cigar butt and narrowed his eyes. He undid his top button and rubbed at his throat as he watched the girl glide by. The way her bottom rolled beneath her thin dress reminded him of a blue-blooded racehorse he owned back in Kentucky. This girl was like that. He smiled to himself. Sleek, seductive and aching to be ridden. A good description.

She was wearing a blue dress that looked as though it might be made of silk the way it clung to her breasts and her bottom. Her bottom seemed to smile at him, her breasts to laugh, jiggling as she sauntered past. He felt a sudden stirring in his groin as he eyed her nipples. He licked his lips. Imagine those lying on your tongue, he thought. Still gripping his cigar in his teeth, he grinned with pleasure.

At a shrewd guess, he thought to himself, that baby isn't wearing any underwear. I could do things with a chick like that.

The ideas grew and what might have been a mere passing fancy solidified with the hardening of his cock and seemed disinclined to leave his brain.

Let's see. Which bit of her do I like the best?

Resting his elbows on the rail of his motor yacht, *Stanza*, he leaned forward, sucking on his cigar and narrowing his eyes some more as he watched the girl walk on by.

'Nice ass,' he murmured. He almost closed his eyes as his imagination took over. He crossed one leg in front of the other in an effort to contain the blood-rush to his lower body.

'Imagine,' he murmured. He clenched and unclenched his hands as if the silkiness of her buttocks were already beneath his palms. Her waist, he decided, was narrow beneath the shapeless shift that she, and most young women like her, wore nowadays. And her breasts. They would be pert and firm, possibly the bits of her he might favour most. Of course, there was also that darker area between her legs, but then, it was such an ambiguous thing, the centre of her sexuality, hidden like a secret temple in a tangled jungle.

'Good job I've got a fine imagination. Fashion!' He chuckled quietly to himself and kept his eyes narrowed against the cigar smoke.

Once she was out of sight, he straightened and took a deep breath.

He looked down at the heaving lump in the front of his trousers.

'You want it, don't you? You want to find your way into that little lady's pussy.'

Smiling, he gave his groin a quick pat.

'Be patient, old friend, and I'll see what I can do.'

Once he had brought himself under some sort of control, he turned and shouted over his shoulder.

'Griffon!'

A man of about six foot four and built like a bull appeared. His eyes were mere black chips in his face. His nose was wide and flat, yet his mouth was small, almost a perfect cupid's bow.

Or a tightly closed asshole, Joe thought to himself.

'Follow that girl, Griffon,' he ordered, nodding in the direction the girl had taken. 'She's wearing a blue silk dress and she's got pale blonde hair. Find out who she is and where she lives, then drop her an invitation. Tell her I'd like her to come and have tea with me this evening.'

'Tea?' Although Griffon's voice sounded questioning, his expression did not change.

Joe smiled knowingly at the man he'd first met in his mother's boarding house in Detroit.

'Have to be careful, Griffon. Tea is an innocent enough place to start with, don't you think?' One blue eye closed in a quick wink. His cigar butt hit the water sizzling, even before Griffon had taken his first step away from the boat.

Unusually swift for a man of his size, he turned away and was off down the gangway and onto the quay, his steps quick though his gait was lumbering as he set off in pursuit of Mariella.

Joseph Michael Carey III smoothed his hair back with hands that were smooth, but not effeminate; large, but not coarse.

Anxiety made him frown as he waited for the girl's response. He hoped she would not be alarmed by Griffon's appearance. What a contrast, he thought to himself; a slender young girl and a lumbering giant like Griffon.

What a contrast also between St Asaph, dreaming away its sunny days and its centuries on the French Riviera, and his mother's boarding house in Detroit.

Like a lot of others, his mother had come from Cracow via Ellis Island. The moment she had arrived, she had made enquiries as to where the most men were working because there an honest woman might make a living too. She did not linger in New York, taking the view that too many immigrants would land there and be disinclined to move on. She had wanted to earn more than just a living. Then she had heard that cities just south of the Great Lakes were the place to be. There had been no plan in her head to go to Detroit, she had just stuck a pin on a map and showed it to the ticket seller at Grand Central Station, New York.

Once she had got to Detroit, sometime in the late 1890s, she had moved in with another woman who kept a boarding house – or at least that was what they had called it.

'Well, ze men they board ze women,' his mother had explained to him in later years. In his young eyes, it had seemed a good enough explanation. Like his name, the words his mother used were agreeable, though not necessarily truthful.

His mother had never married. Like Detroit, she had picked

his name with a pin, but repeated the exercise three times which was why he ended up with 'The Third'.

By the turn of the century, his mother had acquired her own place and by the time he was born, she had more than one such establishment. Of course, she could not help but make a lot of money. As the money accumulated, she had become wary of leaving such amounts in the house. From the very first, she had had good advice. A bank manager, who was also a very good client of hers, advised her to invest, and from just before the turn of the century, she did just that.

'I want to invest in those,' she had said, and had pointed at a shiny, noisy automobile with big brass lights and a noisy horn.

The bank manager had obliged. All the money she had ever made was put into stocks and shares in the burgeoning motor industry.

By the time Joe was in his majority, though unfortunately an orphan, enough wealth had been accumulated to afford him a very luxurious lifestyle.

Joe believed in living life to the full, and being from the background he was, did not feel in the least bit inhibited when it came to sexuality. He was also not terribly honest when it came to collecting beautiful things. He indulged in anything that caught his fancy. The young woman who had glided by earlier had definitely done that.

Chapter 4

The rest of the day Mariella regarded as her own.

The smell of baking bread and fresh fish was left behind as she left the quay and the town behind her. Footsteps light, head full of daydreams, she wandered up a cliff path where mauve and yellow gorse sprouted through tufts of dark green grass.

The path narrowed until it was barely discernible. A small natural alcove had been created by rock and flowering shrubs. Below was the sea, spreading out like a crystallised desert to the blurred horizon.

Stretching her legs out before her, and leaning on her hands, Mariella narrowed her eyes as she looked out at the sea. Her breasts rose and fell as she took deep gulps of salt-laden air.

I feel free, she thought to herself, tossing her hair and tilting her head back so that her face caught the full warmth of the sun.

Because she was feeling like that, and because when she narrowed her eyes the sea really did look like a desert, her mind went back to her unfinished fantasy.

'Valentino,' she whispered. 'My sheik.'

One by one, she undid the buttons at the front of her dress, and dreamlike, took off every other item. Bundled together they made an acceptable pillow. Closing her eyes, she lay back in the crisp, green grass and the sun grew hot on her body.

Arms folded beneath her head, she drifted into her favourite daydream. In her dream, Sahara sand sparkled in the sunlight just like the sea, and the desert sun was just as strong.

In her dream a shadow fell over her. Her heart rate increased as she heard the rustle of desert robes, the sound of leather boots on sand. His face was just as she remembered it; his eyes dark and brooding, his mouth sensuous but with a hint of cruelty.

Her pulse raced as his face came close to hers.

'You are not bending to my will quickly enough,' he said, his breath warm on her face. 'You must learn that I will not be disobeyed. You must learn that I am your master.'

In her fantasy, Mariella's arms were spread out at shoulder level. Her wrists were tied and staked into the desert sand. So too were her legs.

She moaned and writhed against her bonds. 'Please. What are you going to do with me?'

His smile was slow, cruel.

'I am going to leave you staked out here in the sun. Every so often, one of my servants will come out and ascertain whether you are truly broken to my will. He will whip you, beat you in the manner I require.'

'But I will burn,' she protested, suddenly very concerned for her creamy white skin.

He clasped her breast, pinched her nipple as he shook his head.

'Oh no. I will not allow the sun to make your flesh red. I can do that quite well myself.'

Laughing, he got up, the red tassels hanging from the front of his boots swinging as he turned away.

'Let me go,' she cried out. 'Let me go, you barbarian!'

The sheik stopped in his tracks. Slowly, he walked back and stood over her. His dark brow was furrowed. His face was like thunder.

'I will not allow a mere woman to call me a barbarian! But you have called me that. Therefore I think the next stage of your breaking in should start right away.'

Mariella trembled. Although the sun was hot, shivers of fear brought goose bumps onto her flesh.

Eyes wide with dramatic fear, she watched as he loosened a long riding whip from his belt.

He came close, yet she dared not look up at him. She

wanted to close her eyes, but found it impossible. Instead, as her bottom lip trembled, she kept her gaze fixed on the granules of sand that clung to his high leather riding boots.

Soft, yet menacing, the plaited fronds that formed the whip trailed over her cheek.

Mariella gasped and cried out.

'No! Not my face!'

He laughed. 'Of course not your face. I would not like to see that reddened. But,' he snarled, 'I would like to see other parts of your body turning red with my strokes. It is only what you deserve after calling me a barbarian.'

She shivered and her nipples hardened as he trailed the whip over her breasts, poking at her nipples, edging it beneath her breasts and lifting them. Thin but lethal, the soft leather went on to caress her belly.

Hot sunshine did nothing to stop the shivers that coursed through her body. Her mouth hung open as she stared at what the whip was doing.

'Leave me alone,' she cried.

Her cry turned to a moan as the fine end of the whip mixed with her pubic hairs and licked delicately at the beginning of her divide.

Unbearable tingles of delight came into being as the sheik used the whip end to tickle her clitoris.

'No!' She arched her back. Her legs trembled, and the bonds that held her wrists and ankles bit into her flesh as she struggled to escape the delicious sensations.

The whip rose above her, yet even as he brought it down across her belly, the residual feelings it had left between her legs turned pain into a pleasure.

'No!' she cried out, meaning, for him to put it back where it was.

'No!' The sheik's dark eyes turned darker. 'You do not say that word to me. Do you understand?'

Mariella was not really listening, so her answer was still in response to what she was feeling, not what she was hearing.

'No!' she cried out again.

His face came close to hers. Eyes bleary with delight, she looked up into its craggy attractiveness, smelt him, wanted to reach out and touch him.

'No is a word you will not use!' he warned.

Mariella, wanting him to touch her, yet wanting to defy him, watched as he passed the whip into his left hand and retrieved a smaller, more delicate whip from his waistband.

As it dangled before her eyes, she took a deep breath. Granted it was smaller than the other whip which was obviously used to stir a horse to greater effort. But this one was different.

Three leather strips hung from its end. On the end of each was a ball of what looked like some kind of thistle.

Mesmerised with fear, Mariella sucked in her breath, her heart thumping as she watched it come closer.

'This,' he hissed, 'will make your breasts red. The pain it causes will not be sharp, but your beautiful flesh will itch and tingle with the kiss of its tiny spikes. Now. Will you submit to my will?'

'No!' shouted Mariella, her eyes fixed on the strange whip.

He knelt at her side, and with great deliberation brought the torturous balls of thistles down onto the first breast.

It tingled at first. Then it burnt.

She whimpered, her eyes following its progress as he raised it, the whip and his form dark against the sky.

The effect was incredible. She arched her back and gasped each time the prickly balls landed on her breasts. With each stroke the sheik ensured that at least one thistle landed on her nipple.

He alternated between breasts, his kohl-lined eyes glowing with pleasure as her breasts changed colour.

She trembled, jerked and twisted her body as she fought to get away from the tingling strokes.

Satisfaction in his smile, the sheik paused. Bending down, he stroked each breast.

'They are tender now,' he murmured. His eyes burned with excitement.

Hers burnt with defiance. She bit her bottom lip to stop from crying out.

She smelt the exotic oils of his hair as his lips kissed her breasts. Softly, his mouth circled her nipples, his kisses delicate as well as determined. Flesh tingling, she shuddered.

'Now,' he murmured, his voice husky with desire, 'perhaps you will at last submit to my will.'

Chapter 5

Hans van der Loste, whose brilliantly white motor yacht *Cartouche* was moored next to *Stanza*, Joe Carey's yacht, was reading a newspaper when Mariella walked by. Prior to his valet handing him the paper, the man had sewn its pages into place with white cotton, and then pressed it with a warm iron. Hans van der Loste was a man of meticulous tastes.

At first his eyes had slid sideways to study the young woman from behind the darkness of his sunglasses. Then, on deciding that she was worth more than a passing glance, he slid his sunglasses up onto his head and let his newspaper slide into his lap.

'What would you do for one of my diamonds,' he mused softly to himself. His eyes fastened on the bouncing of her breasts as she strode, young and beautiful, along the sun-baked quay.

Like a gazelle, he thought to himself. You move like a gazelle.

He turned his head so he could more easily follow her progress. He had no need to get out of his chair. It was easy enough to study her shape and the sway of her body through the white railings of his yacht. Besides, he was sure he would see her again.

Not a local, he mused to himself. She is far too well dressed to be the daughter of some fisherman who has turned to running a waterside café or restaurant. This is a classy woman. A visitor. And what else is there for a beautiful woman to do but to promenade, and who can resist the smell of the sea and the sound of seagulls crying?

'And when I see you again,' he murmured softly to himself, 'perhaps we will see what you will do for a diamond.'

Hans van der Loste removed his sunglasses from his crisp, blond hair. He put both them and the newspaper onto the table in front of him. Then he lay back, clasped his hands before his chin, and closed his eyes.

I would imagine you would do quite a bit for a diamond, he mused to himself. Merely thinking the word made the jewels appear in his head. Diamonds of all shapes and sizes sparkled behind his closed eyelids, moving in spectacular patterns like those in a child's kaleidoscope. But in the midst of those beautiful gems, he could see a woman's body. For a moment, he thought he could also see pink diamonds among the white. He was mistaken. The pinkness was her nipples. As her breasts rose, the diamonds that had been piled over her body, slid away. Only those on her belly remained, including one that was set into her navel. Below these, he could see her pubic lips which were shiny and completely devoid of hair.

'I like that,' he exclaimed softly, and what he said was indeed the truth. Hans liked things clean. Smooth. He liked them precise, and he liked them to shine. Anything that was shiny was of interest. Gold, gems, and beautiful women. Those were the things that interested Hans van der Loste, a man from Amsterdam who dealt in all things of value.

His family had been wealthy too, and they had also been indulgent. Unlike the English, Hans was not sent away to school but supplemented the provision of a tutor at home with day attendance at a very good Jesuit college.

Hans had also had other education at home. His father, a man of diverse tastes, had also supplied his son with a non-academic education. This had come in the form of Lizel, a girl with warm brown eyes and a warmer bosom who also doubled as a chambermaid, mostly in his father's chamber.

Because of his fastidiousness, Hans had insisted his own bath was filled for Lizel to use prior to him using her. As she bathed, he would sit and watch her, his youthful erection growing as she soaped her glistening breasts and sponged her nipples which were bigger and browner than her eyes.

He had also insisted that all body hair be removed and had watched on each of the occasions his valet had lathered and shaved the girl. Once that had been done, he would have her scented all over with a particular cream his father had acquired.

Once all was complete, he would sniff her all over, revelling in the delightful mix of perfume, body and softness.

His partiality for such a mix had never left him.

But he was a patient man. He sincerely believed that all good things come to those who wait.

Chapter 6

They were in Mariella's hotel room and Peter was sitting in a pink and brown tub chair with black metal arms. His voice was slow, almost menacing.

'So the American has invited you for tea.' A cynical smile curled around Peter's lips. Some women would have recoiled at such a smile. Mariella did not. On the contrary, the hint of mocking wickedness sent tantalising sensations down her back and over her breasts and belly. Like an unseen phantom, they accumulated between her legs; made her want to groan but also made her want to scream.

'I'm looking forward to it.'

Smoke curled from a Turkish cigarette. As if disdainful of its sting, Peter narrowed his eyes and continued to gaze at Mariella.

Mariella walked slowly around the room, her movements slow, enticing. She smiled at him over her shoulder. 'Are you jealous?'

He shook his head slowly without his eyes ever leaving her body. His thumb was against his lips. The smoke curled up over it.

His eyes continued to scrutinise her body as if he were looking for some flaw, some part of her that was not quite to his taste.

Such scrutiny made her tingle.

Having just got out of her bath, her skin was slightly pink and still warm from the water. An amused smile played around her red lips. Her eyes twinkled in an innocent kind of way that made her look foolishly girlish.

With obvious intent, she moved slowly, dabbing at her skin as she turned. Sometimes her bottom was towards him and sometimes her belly. Either way, she would raise her leg onto a convenient chair and bend over to dry her toes.

At last she lost interest in trying to imagine what he was thinking. What did it matter? After all, it was no more than a game, another game like so many others they played.

Standing up straight, she flung the towel to one side and tossed her chin-length bob away from her face. Petulance clouded her features, yet the urge to make him jealous would not go away.

'Do you think it will only be tea he offers me?'

Peter raised his chin. 'I hope not.'

There was a touch of arrogance in his voice and in the aristocratic way he tossed his head.

'That is not why I want you to accept his invitation. You are there for a purpose. You are there to do my will. I hope you will enjoy more than tea. You cannot find out secrets if he only gives you tea.'

She stood before him as he sat in the chair. He continued to smoke. She felt he was daring her to do more.

And I want to do more, she thought. I cannot help but want to do more. That is the effect this Russian aristo has on me. He commands and I obey no matter what he asks of me. Yet even if he plays with me too roughly, in too self-centred a way, I still view him with joy for his lovemaking stuns me.

Masking her thoughts but smiling provocatively, she dropped to her knees between his. She ran her hands up and down his thighs and felt his muscles bunch beneath her touch.

'And you are sure he has the icon you seek?'

Her dark lashes swept her cheek as she looked up at him through a shock of silvery blonde hair that had fallen over her eyes.

'There is no doubt. Vladimir, my father's cousin, brought it out of Russia. But as I have already explained, he was a foolish man. At the hotel in Prague where he was staying, he got to talking and drinking with wealthy men. That was where he handed over the icon. These two are those men.

Vladimir was loose-tongued. He talked of the icon. One of those men has it, but both deny it. I leave it to you to find out which one.'

Still on her knees, Mariella stretched forward so that her hands rested on his hips. Her eyes went to the junction between his thighs.

Transfixed, she watched his fingers moving over his groin, then settling to caress his hardening prick. She felt his eyes upon her, yet could not look at him. Her gaze was fixed on the way he was touching himself. The slowness and deliberation of his fingers were so hypnotic, she almost began to feel jealous.

When he at last undid his trousers and brought out his big, virile member, her mouth dropped open and a gasp of anticipation fled from her throat.

Contemplating what was to come, she licked her bottom lip. So wet was her tongue that her lip was left as shiny pink and as moist as the pinkness hidden between her legs. Unblinking, her gaze remained fixed on the item before her.

A thumping came to her chest, an ache to her groin. She needed his fingers there. Needed his prick there. Before she could make the first move to get the scenario under way, Peter spoke first.

'Pleasure me,' he ordered. 'And later when you sip your tea with your American gentleman, taste also what you will take from me.'

Cigarette extinguished, Peter used both hands to grip her wrists and clamp them to the chair arms.

Wide eyed, she stared at the bonds that her dark-eyed lover was tying around her wrists. The hard metal of the chair arms was cold beneath her flesh.

A glimmer of fantasy entered her mind. Would Valentino do this? Would her sheik force her into such a perverted act?

The answer made her tremble. She gazed into Peter's face, imagined him robed, his face half hidden.

She was no longer interested in what he had used to bind

her. Just as he had intended, all her attention was fixed on what he wanted her to do.

A deep thrill seemed to weave down the bones of her spine. At the same time, his hands smoothed her hair back from her face so he could see more clearly what she was doing.

'Take me,' he ordered.

She gave him no resistance as he pressed on the back of her head so that her face went forward. Masculine scent covered her nose and pubic hair grated gently against her chin. Lips and teeth parted. She took him in.

Every trick he had taught her was brought into use. Her tongue licked over his flesh, moistening his shaft and his glans. Whimpering as she sucked on him, she also wriggled her bottom as if to tempt him to push his foot between her legs, to bring off the orgasm that hung there like heavy jewels.

Peter did no such thing. He was in complete control, his hands manipulating her head to whatever tempo he chose. Sometimes he used her head slowly so that her lips merely caressed his stem and the merest hint of fluid placed flavour on her tongue. To suit himself, he increased the speed, the tempo fast, furious as though he were very angry with her and would spear her with the rod of flesh.

Eventually, the tempo hastened for the very last time. He held her head firm, her lips tight against his pubic hair.

At the same time, his half-buried prick delivered a quantity of semen that was as great as his climax. His warmth trickled down into her body like mulled wine or cream laced both with sugar and with salt. He held her there until the last drop had left him, then he eased her back so she could lick all stickiness away from him.

'What about me?' she asked him.

He cupped her face in his palms and gazed into her eyes.

'Are you in great need of release?'

She wriggled against him, her breasts now caught between his knees. She held her head back so that her throat was exposed and looked at him along the lines of her nose.

'You know I am.' Her voice was hushed though strangely strong. 'I need it.'

He smiled and nodded in that slow way of his that sometimes irritated and sometimes excited her. His lips were soft and warm as he kissed her forehead, her nose, her chin.

'And that is how you should be. Think of how aroused you will be sitting there sipping tea. At the same time as tasting the tea, you will be tasting my come. Think of how hot your pussy will be feeling because I have aroused you and given you no release.'

Mariella closed her eyes and saw the desert, her sheik, and the things he did to her. She groaned as she opened her eyes.

'You are cruel, Peter Stavorsky.'

He took her chin in his hand. 'And you love it, Mariella. You're living a fantasy. You adore fantasies and you adore adventure.'

Mariella mewed and rubbed her breasts against him. Her need was urgent, but she took his point. Storing up her desire would make the act that much better.

'Are you sure this man Carey will oblige me?'

Her hips undulated. The ache in her loins was almost a torture, though a piquant, delightful one.

Smiling, Peter shook his head and smoothed her hair away from her face as he had before. 'How could he resist?'

Mariella nestled her head in his groin and closed her eyes. In her mind, the sheik had turned her over on her bed of sand.

Sand grated against her breasts and belly as the first whip landed on her buttocks until they became more red than the sun could make them.

Then he used the thistle balls between her open legs and caused her sex to burn with desire.

Chapter 7

The best hotel in St Asaph overlooked the wide quay and the road that ran from the fishermen's cottages at one end to the headland at the other. It was called La Grande Sophie, owned by a man seldom seen who few people could describe in any great detail.

Claude Doriere watched life from the penthouse suite at the top of the hotel he owned, a suite fashioned mostly from glass. The glass construction was seemingly held in place by sentinels fashioned in an Art Deco style, a design based on statues associated with Nineveh or ancient Ur.

Placed like a defensive cannon before a wide glass window in his isolated eerie, was a brass and ebony telescope. With the aid of this telescope, Claude kept in touch with everything that went on in the exclusive resort on the Côte d'Azure, and there was nothing that much surprised him about the place.

On this particular day, his gaze lingered on the delightful form of a fair-haired girl in a blue dress, her long legs striding along the quay as if inviting a man to give chase. The way she walked enthralled him. Not only that, but he found that if he held the telescope at a certain angle to the sun, he could see the shape of her body beneath the flimsy material of her dress.

Unable to resist, he followed her with his telescopic eye and would have continued to do so, if a sudden movement hadn't attracted his attention. A large man was running after the girl. At first he thought some dark motive might have been intended and wished immediately that he was near enough to intervene. Then he saw the girl stop and turn. They appeared to talk before the man went his way and she went hers.

It was only after the girl was out of sight that he trained his telescope in the other direction to follow the man. He saw him go aboard one of the finest yachts moored at the quay, a three-masted brig named *Stanza*. He saw him talk to a young man wearing a silk shirt and creamy linen trousers. The clothes were the sort only bought in the best shops of Paris or Rome and were worn with an air of casual indifference. As though such things had no real value.

Just then, as the young man ran his hand over his neat hairstyle, Claude saw the glint of sunlight on gold as something slid up the young man's wrist. He recognised what it was immediately. Nothing glinted quite like quality.

This young man, he decided, was a connoisseur of all things of value; all things beautiful. Including the girl, he thought to himself.

Another movement caught his eye. The owner of the next yacht was sliding sunglasses down onto the sort of nose that completes a classic profile. His hair was so fair as to be almost blindingly white.

'He too has been eyeing the girl,' Claude chuckled. This was a man he knew. 'Hans van der Loste,' he said quietly to himself. 'Now you really are a man with a twenty-carat taste.'

Claude let the telescope swivel on its brackets as he walked back into the room.

He glanced back as the image of the girl came to his mind. Her looks had entranced, and he had loved the dreamy, faraway look in her eyes.

What had she been thinking, he wondered, as she walked so provocatively along the wide quay that ran beside the luxury vessels?

'You cannot know,' he said to himself as he opened a wardrobe door, then opened a door to a secret cupboard beyond that. 'But you want to find out.'

He ran his hands over the varied items hanging there. Some were quite well made; suits in loud checks that a loud man might wear. A cardinal's outfit; a sea captain's. Beside the opulent, there were also the more lowly. The brown robes of a lowly friar, the rough-edged clothing of a fisherman, and the neater attire of a humble waiter.

He paused, his hand on the latter. Brushing fluff from the shoulder as he took it out, he smiled, then hung it on a hook in the outer wardrobe.

'This, I think, is exactly what is required – at least for the moment.'

He sighed, then his hands worked fast. He took off his own clothes; the Egyptian cotton shirt, the French silk tie, the Savile Row business suit.

Thoughtfully, he ran his hands over the uniform of a waiter, as worn by those working in his own hotel.

Chapter 8

Mariella dressed carefully for her tea-time appointment with Joseph Michael Carey III. The hem of the pretty yellow dress she wore barely reached her knees, but its scantiness was tempered by the sweeping chiffon of its handkerchief corners that were weighted with cute, gold tassels.

The feel of the dress delighted her. So fine was the fabric, so delicate the weave, she might just as easily have been naked.

'How do I look?' she asked Peter.

His deep, hooded eyes scrutinised her in much the same way as a vulture examines its next meal. His smile was slow, his voice effective.

'Irresistible. You will definitely receive more than tea!'

Her hair gleamed, her eyes sparkled, their blueness accentuated by the smoky haze of the makeup on her eyelids.

Peter granted her the use of the Lagonda and his chauffeur to take her to the quay and Carey's gleaming white yacht. Like its owner, the car sounded provocative, its engine a deep hum that only hinted at its power.

Because it was spring and they were bordering the Mediterranean, sunset was not too distant when she arrived at the quay.

The young American awaited her, his face bright with excitement.

'I'm sure glad you could come,' he said as she stepped aboard. 'Joseph Michael Carey III.'

The hand that shook hers was warm, the grip firm. As though I were an old school chum, she thought, or a friend come to play tennis.

'Mariella,' she answered with an engaging smile.

'Mariella what?'

Her smile became a laugh. She tossed her head in an off-hand manner and turned away. 'Just Mariella.'

His smile and laugh seemed all mixed up into one. It was contagious and she couldn't help responding.

Why was it, she asked herself, that Americans had such teeth? So white. So unblemished.

He escorted her to the aft deck where tea was already laid on the sort of folding table that some people use to play cards on. The chairs were of that type too; the folding type with green canvas backs and seats.

'Well!' he said as he plumped himself down in a chair. 'It sure is nice to have you here.'

Mariella sat opposite him.

'Yes.' Her fingers started a nervous tapping, but she managed to control it.

The tea lay untouched. For what seemed minutes but was probably only seconds, she admired his bronzed complexion and the way his hair refused to be neat and drifted down over his eyes.

Obviously, he saw her look. As if guilty about it, his hand went up to push it back again.

Mariella sat very upright. The neckline of her dress swooped low over her breasts. She instinctively knew he was admiring her, imagining his lips kissing her throat and running down to that indentation where her collarbone divided.

Men can be predictable, she thought, and that can be sad.

'Well!' she exclaimed. 'This is nice.'

'Yes,' he replied, seemingly as tongue-tied as her.

She folded her hands into her lap and licked at her lips. She eyed the tea things and as she licked her lips again, she thought about what Peter had said – about her tasting his semen as she sipped her tea.

She made an instant decision. With a sigh and a sudden quick movement, she crossed one leg over the other and moved forwards.

'Shall I pour?'

Their fingers touched as he took the cup from her. His hand shook. Mariella merely smiled.

'So how long are you staying?' he asked as he put the cup to his lips. She saw him wince as the tea hit his tongue.

'Did you want sugar? Milk?'

He shook his head. 'It doesn't matter. I'm only interested in knowing more about you.'

Mariella was slow in replying, savouring her tea and closing her eyes each time she took a sip. After each sip, she rolled her tongue along her bottom lip and flicked it languidly over the corners of her mouth.

Peter was right, she thought to herself. The swine. Even at a distance I still feel him.

She smiled reassuringly at her host. Perhaps influenced by lustful thoughts, she saw his thigh muscles tense beneath the fine linen trousers that might have been fashioned in Paris, London or Rome.

'I asked how long you were staying.' He paused, looking unsure as to whether she had heard him. She let him flounder, his eyes moving rapidly, his hands quivering as he sought a different tack. 'Mariella. It's a lovely name for a lovely girl.'

There! It was out. He had made the first move. Mariella sighed with satisfaction. Like chess, it was an opening gambit. Now it was up to her to give the right response, one he could build his attack on.

She laughed before speaking and could see from the sudden fire in his eyes that he found it seductive. She rearranged herself in the chair, crossed one silk stockinged leg over the other, fully aware that the sensuality of her movements would eventually lead him into temptation.

'But you don't know I'm lovely. You don't know either my mind or my body, Joseph.' Seduction was in her voice, in her eyes. She was tempting him with every asset available.

'Joe. Call me Joe.' Relief seemed to rush across his face. 'I know of no reason why I shouldn't get to know either your mind or your body better than I do.'

He smiled in a disarming way. The breeze blew his hair across his eyes and he brushed it back without his gaze leaving her. An innocent act, she thought. Part of his charm, she guessed. Appear boyish, appear innocent, and the rest is easy. Someone had told him that at some time; possibly a woman.

'She seduces you without the need to seduce her. Or at least, she meets you half-way.' Good advice whoever had said it.

Joe stood up, and as he did so the wind took his hair again and tossed it carelessly across his brow. Without bothering to rearrange it this time, he narrowed his eyes and looked towards the west.

'The sun's setting.' An obvious statement. He shoved his hands in his pockets and sucked on his bottom lip. 'Shall we sail out there to see it melt into the sea?' He nodded towards the horizon that seemed trimmed with salmon pink.

Somehow the suggestion was unexpected, even romantic. But Mariella showed no surprise, though she did show her pleasure. She smiled and uttered a soft 'yes'.

The silky softness of her dress rustled as she got to her feet. The chiffon that fell in soft diagonals lifted in the breeze that blew off the sea. Her movements were purposeful, yet startlingly seductive.

'I'd love that,' she said and braced her legs as the breeze blew under her dress and around the naked area of thigh between stocking tops and knickers.

She liked the way he looked at her. For the first time she noticed his eyebrows were darker than his hair and that a woman could be jealous of the length of his lashes.

'Then I'll arrange it,' he said, his voice tinged with excitement. 'And out there in the sunset, I'll get to know you better.'

He disappeared for a moment between the mahogany-lined walls of the yacht's interior.

Mariella, congratulating herself that things were going her way, made her way to the ship's rail. One hand on the rail, she poked at the corners of her mouth with her small finger. Not that her lipstick was smudged. She was doing it purely to hide the peel of triumphant laughter that threatened to come from her throat.

She shrugged her shoulders to her ears. 'This is exciting!' she exclaimed, her eyes sparkling.

Joe reappeared with several members of the crew. One among them shouted orders. A few of the men glanced her way before hauling aloft the sail.

An engine throbbed to life beneath her feet.

'It's just to get us out of harbour,' Joe explained on seeing her surprised expression.

Orders for ropes to be loosened and the engine to be reversed and then changed into forward were given.

As they moved away from the quay, a host of seagulls took off from the fishing boats they passed, their screams almost mocking, a high, corrupted laughter.

'Who's at the helm?' she asked him.

He pointed to the wheel. 'My captain,' he explained. 'There's an internal wheel house as well, but it's a fair evening. He and two deck hands will stay up here with us, though of course, they will not see us. We will have our privacy.'

His lips were close and she could read the look in his eyes.

'It's a beautiful sight,' Mariella said, tilting her head back as she gazed at the flapping sheets above her.

'Like you,' he whispered.

His breath was slightly moist and warm on her ear. She turned to face him, knowing what was coming next and fully intending to do anything he wanted to do.

Seagulls dipped and dived over the yacht's wake as they kissed.

She felt the warmth of his hands through her dress, smelt the delicious, masculine smell that was indefinable, so individual to each and every man.

And yet, she was not as aroused as she should be. How could she possibly get close to him, find out about Peter's icon if she wasn't going to enjoy sex with him?

You could fake it, she told herself.

No! No you couldn't. If you faked it, it would mean you weren't enjoying it. That wouldn't be fair. Peter still might get his icon, but what would you be getting out of it?

If only he had dark hair and deep brown eyes, she thought to herself.

She closed her eyes, and as his smell invaded her senses, she imagined his blue eyes had changed to brown and his hair had become as dark as his lashes.

'Kiss me like Valentino,' she pleaded. 'Hold me tightly, so tight that it hurts!'

'Oh, yes,' murmured Joe, thinking she was merely lost in passion and not imagining herself with someone else. 'Like this?'

'Cruelly,' cried Mariella between kisses. 'Fiercely.'

Joe's biceps felt like iron against her shoulders as he clasped her closer. His mouth bruised her lips; his teeth were hard against hers, and his tongue plunged into her mouth.

'My sheik,' she murmured, her eyes still closed.

In her mind she was cruising the Nile, a Sahara breeze caressing her body, the smell of old wood, rope and sweat mixed with the sound of rushing water. And he was there, her sheik, his body hard, his eyes unforgiving and ever demanding.

Fantasy ignited a sweet ache hidden deep in her body. From its depth, it spread out like lengths of silk thread, touching each and every nerve in her body.

Her belly wanted him. Her arms wanted him, and her nipples flagrantly hardened as they pushed into his chest.

'It's a beautiful sunset,' he said to her without even looking to the west. 'It's made your face turn pink. Like naked flesh. I bet you'd turn pink all over.'

Opening her eyes could not be avoided. Desire lessened once she could see that Joe looked nothing like her movie idol. Yet she could not stop. Not now. Her mission was on the way to being accomplished.

'Will they see?' she asked indicating the three members of crew who were still on deck.

'Does it matter?'

Her gaze slid to the three men. One had his back towards them, but she instinctively knew the other two were watching out of the corners of their eyes.

'No,' she replied, a new flowering of desire rising in her loins. She smiled directly at him. 'I shall pretend I'm a great movie star and am purely doing this for my art.'

'What?' Joe stared at her open mouthed.

Still smiling, but more coquettishly now, Mariella slipped off her dress and let it fall with a soft rustle to lie around her ankles.

A sigh of longing turned into a groan as it left the lips of the youthful American. 'You are pink,' he said as his eyes raked over her.

Posing as only a truly sexual creature knows how, Mariella stood there. She wore nothing but her stockings, a pair of pink silk garters, pink underwear, and the long length of jet beads that had originally been over the yellow dress.

'Come here.' His voice was little above a whisper. Fingers tightening around her bead necklace, he pulled her to him.

Eyes wide, mouth open, he gazed spellbound at her breasts. The beads were still in his hands, tangled around his fingers. Childish fascination on his face, he wound them around each orb in turn.

'They're trapped,' he said with an amused grin as he used the beads to pull her breasts upwards. His eyes began to sparkle.

Mariella, frequently casting her gaze in the direction of the two crew members, blushed with excitement. She was surprised at how she was feeling. For the most part, things were exactly as Peter had said they would be. And yet, they were more than that.

Being watched excited her. Besides that, who would have thought that a string of jet beads could be used to stimulate her?

Closing her eyes, she rested her hands on his shoulders and felt his muscles tense beneath her touch.

Breathing heavily, he bent his head to suck on each stiff nipple.

Mariella buried her nose in his hair. Her cries were laced with whimpers of pleasure.

Through half-closed eyes, she saw the two crewmen. They stood completely still, mesmerised by what they were seeing.

Mariella imagined they were Arabs, subjects of the desert sheik who continuously invaded her night-time sleep and her daydreams.

If she concentrated really hard, she could imagine that the village clinging to the shore was really Casablanca or Tunis. And if she really put her mind to it, she could imagine that the tongue licking at her nipples belonged to her sheik who was really an American film star known by women the world over as Valentino.

Inspired by her fertile imagination, when he kissed her again, she forced her tongue between his lips, licked the roof of his mouth and his pure white teeth. Inwardly she laughed and wondered whether he could taste the semen on her tongue as much as she could. What would he say if he knew that the residue of another man's seed was within his mouth?

But Mariella would not allow him to stop. Her head was reeling as her mind danced between the erotic sex of her dreams, and the equally erotic encounter of the moment.

Excited to fever pitch, she ran her hands down over Joe's crisp white shirt and moaned with desire. There was something provocative about feeling muscular outlines beneath a layer of crisp cotton. Desire rising, she followed the indentation of his spine all the way down to the waistband of his trousers.

Whilst rubbing her nipples against his chest, she slid one finger into the start of the crease that divided his buttocks, then brought her hands back up.

His kiss, the feel of his shirt against her bare breasts made her feel as though she were burning. Through his shirt, she felt the warmth of his back, smooth and hard beneath her touch.

Consumed with longing, she began to pull the Sea Island cotton from out of his trousers.

Breath racing, he helped her, pulling at the front of his shirt so it flapped like a depleted sail around him.

'Oh my love,' she gasped, her eyes closed as she rubbed her cheek against his chest. 'I always knew you'd have a body like this beneath those long robes. Smooth skin. Hard flesh.'

'Robes?' He sounded surprised.

'Clothes! I meant your clothes.'

It took effort, but she managed to pull herself back from her fantasy world just enough to convince him that it was he she was thinking of. Actions, she decided, would speak louder than words.

Feverish with kisses, with words and with actions, she almost tore the buttons from his trousers, and when at last the hot, pulsating length was in her hand, she moaned against his throat that she had to have it.

'I've been denied it for far too long!' she exclaimed.

Joe gasped. 'Do you mean you've never . . .' His voice trailed away as the prospect hit him. 'Do you mean you're still a . . .'

An open mouth and a lip that shuddered obliterated the suave sophistication of the man born of a poor Polish immigrant.

He's smitten, thought Mariella. In order that she might

enjoy her sojourn with him more effectively, she floated back into her fantasy world where the man of her dreams was dark, not fair, and had brown eyes, not blue. However, she was alert enough to notice that his cock leapt more strongly from his crotch. Now, she decided, is the time to begin our relationship.

'Please,' she whimpered against his ear, eyelids shining with dusky blue makeup. 'Please. Don't keep me waiting any longer.'

Inspired by what he believed, Joe groaned.

'Will you let me do everything?' he asked, his voice husky with passion.

'Anything you want.'

Again he groaned, his penis leaping in his pants at the prospect of sex without limitations.

His hands slid down to rest on her behind, his fingers exploring everywhere he wanted.

'I can't believe this,' he murmured. 'This is so wonderful. I haven't had a woman behave like this since back in my youth in Chicago. And she sure was no virgin!'

Mariella only murmured unintelligible words. Joe was arousing her, yet he could not know that he was merely an aid to her fantasy.

In her mind she was stretched out on silken cushions in the middle of a cage. Wrists and ankles chafed against the iron fetters that held her. Naked and vulnerable, her body writhed, her hips undulated as if trying to escape whatever was in store for her. But there was no escape, and she didn't want there to be any.

Beyond the bars of the cage were the red and black drapes of the Bedouin tent. Smoke from burning incense swayed and circled up into the air.

Everything was exactly as she had expected it to be. All she wanted now was the object of her fantasy, the man who thrilled her through and through.

At last she saw him. The sheik was on the outside of the

cage. She could see his eyes through the bars. They were full of fire and made her tingle with apprehension.

Arms folded, head held high, he stood back and waited as one of his henchmen unlocked the cage.

As he walked towards her, her gaze slid to the red tassels swinging like pendulums from his high leather boots. Her gaze stayed on them until she could summon up the courage to look up into his eyes. When she did, she trembled.

Dark and disdainful, he stood looking down at her, his jaw rigid, his mouth unsmiling. Suddenly, a dark scowl crossed his face. His hands went to the front of the black outfit he wore.

Mariella's eyes opened wide. Her breath seemed to catch in her throat. This was the moment! This was when it was going to happen.

Then she saw him smile, heard him laugh.

'But I don't want to be blindfolded,' she protested. 'I want to see your body.'

The words stayed in her mind. On her tongue they were merely a series of sighs, groans and mumbled utterances.

Reality came creeping into her daydream. Her fantasy began to fade.

She became vaguely aware that someone was muttering something against her ear, but she wasn't sure quite who it was.

'We'll do it to suit you,' Joe murmured. 'I think that would be best.'

Mariella drifted back from her fantasy. His comment puzzled her, but her imagined moment with her sheik had done its work. She was now too impassioned to bother about questioning him.

Prick standing proud and a dark gleam in his blue eyes, Joe sat himself in one of the canvas chairs.

'There,' he said breathlessly as he held his member steady with both hands. 'I told you today would be a good day. I told you you'd get what you deserved, boy.'

Amused as well as amazed, Mariella glanced from Joe's face to his cock.

She opened her mouth, about to ask did he always speak to his penis on such a personal basis, but not wishing to waste the chance of a good thing, she changed her mind.

'Shall I do it like this?' she asked him, eyes wide with innocence and legs wide in order to accommodate him.

'Oh yeah, baby,' he moaned, his gaze fixed on her opening lips. Opening like the petals of a dark, purple tulip, her sex became like the head of a flower and fitted over the tip of his stem.

A long, low moan escaped from her throat. She closed her eyes as she braced her hands on the chair arms and slowly slid down the whole length of his shaft until it was completely buried inside her.

'You took it very easily. You must be a natural.'

Joe sounded surprised and she wondered why.

'Of . . . course . . . I . . . am,' she responded, her words interspersed by sharp intakes of breath.

'I've got myself a substantial prick and I have every intention of enjoying it to the full.'

As she began to thud up and down on his cock, Joe reached for her breasts.

At times he encompassed each breast in the palm of his hands. Tiring of that, he varied his attentions by pinching her nipples, flicking at them with his fingernails, or pulling on them until they seemed stretched to twice their normal length.

No matter what he did, nothing could put Mariella off her stroke. Each action only caused the ache that had been in her belly to whirl off into a myriad sensations. It was as though her whole body were a conductor for every sexual sensation that had ever existed.

Her mind too was playing the same game. She did not doubt now that Joe was the man within her, yet there was one small corner where the sheik still dominated. This time he seemed only at a distance; a black and white effigy on a silver screen, threatening his co-star with a fate worse than death.

Worse! Was he crazy!

In Mariella's opinion, nothing could be better than submitting to a man like Valentino. Let it all happen, she thought to herself. Let me have it all, and let me enjoy it all.

She could hear the wetness of her own juices squelching between him and her. Trickles of it ran between her buttocks before transferring to his balls. She guessed their subtle trickle would be pleasant for him.

'Is . . . it . . . good?' he asked between each thump of her sex against his.

Her eyes were closed and her lips were pursed. The sound she made was like a kettle does when it's about to boil.

'I . . . am . . . coming,' she said between each of her actions.

To Joe, it was almost as if she had pressed a secret button. Because she had told him she was coming, his own body seemed to want to join her in her pleasure. Besides that, he was ecstatic that a woman who he had presumed to be a virgin had the capacity to enjoy sex right from the very first time. He had, he thought, a right to be congratulated. He had brought her off. Her, a virgin.

A virgin! A virgin! A virgin!

The words thudded in his brain in time with her sex thudding against him.

The thought of having been the first to breach her hymen added impetus to his arousal. Once it reached boiling point, his semen shot up through his stem.

'Wonderful!' he shouted as he thrust his pelvis up to meet her.

'Don't stop!' she cried, moaning as she rode him fast, slow, before she seemed to waver, spasm and finally sigh as she fell over him. She leaned her head against his so that her breasts were not far from his mouth.

'That was wonderful,' she said between kisses. Her fingers drew circles, lines and triangles in his hair.

Joe sighed. 'Gee, that's great. And I didn't hurt you?'

Hands clasped around his neck, she looked at him quizzically. 'Hurt me! Why should you have hurt me?'

Joe suddenly felt an utter fool. Had he really been that mistaken?

'You mean you weren't a virgin?'

Mariella laughed. She was about to call him a fool when a sudden thought came to her. Her laugh subsided. After all, it might be very beneficial to the cause of her lover, Peter, to have this lanky American think he had awakened her sexuality.

'I enjoyed it,' she said sweetly. 'Do you think you could teach me some more things like that?'

Joe's apprehension disappeared. His white teeth flashed against his bronze tan. 'Sure,' he said with obvious enthusiasm. 'Sure I can. Shall we do some more tonight?'

Mariella smiled as she nodded. Out of the corner of her eye she could see the two crew members who had been watching them.

They were now hanging out over the sea. With one hand they were holding onto a halyard. With the other they were pulling on their pricks and jettisoning showers of semen into the sea.

Chapter 9

So powerful was Claude Doriere's telescope that he had easily detected the copulating silhouette against the pinkness of the sunset. With avid enthusiasm and a sense of participation, he had watched and smiled.

'What an enthusiastic young woman,' he exclaimed.

His comment was sincere. Nothing pleased him so well as a job well done and a performance worth watching. And this was a performance, wasn't it? Didn't each lover try to impress the other with their sensuality, their ability both to receive and to give pleasure?

I wonder if she desires that young American for himself or for his money? he thought, as he began to retract the brass and ebony instrument.

Tonight was the night when he had planned to refocus his telescope so he could study the angle of Venus with Orion. After retracting the telescope, he began turning the controls that would readjust the finely made instrument. Before pulling out the retractable extension, he checked the focus, training the lens along the dark horizon, then bringing it back to skim the quiet quay. That was when he spotted another interesting character. The man was leaning against one of the lampposts that now lined the quay; three white spheres atop an ornate cast iron post. The lights had only been put up in the last five years. These new lights owed more to aesthetic considerations rather than practical. Like a string of pearls spewed up by the heaving sea, they lined the quay and took the eye around the bay to where the headland jutted away from the land, shielding St Asaph from the rest of the world.

But Claude Doriere was not interested in how pretty the

glowing globes shone in the gathering dusk. He was more interested in the character who leaned aginst that one lamp.

There was something familiar about the man, though that was not necessarily any big surprise. After all, Claude spent a lot of his time spying on the town he had come to regard as his own. 'Probably a local fisherman – or more likely a café proprietor,' he pronounced disdainfully, correcting the sentence when he remembered that most fishermen had left the sea and become involved in catering.

As the man came into better focus, Claude changed his opinion. His clothes were too good for either a fisherman or a café proprietor. Fairly tall and of athletic proportions, his hair was dark as were the clothes he wore. Even before the man turned round, Claude knew instinctively that his eyebrows would be bushy and meet just above the bridge of his nose. There would also be a surly look about him. He was the sort who snapped like a catfish if you happened to use the wrong words or looked at him the wrong way.

A dull ache came to Claude's stomach. Faded with time, but still painful, old memories came back to haunt him. He did his best to sift through them, to snatch this man's details from the history of his own life.

'I know you,' he said in a hushed tone, a worried frown on his face. 'But from where?'

His hands tensed over the wheels that manoeuvred the telescope. This man, he was sure, was not a local. He had seen him elsewhere in the world. Deep in his memory was the knowledge that whatever the man had been or had been doing was not necessarily either legal or savoury.

Being a well-travelled man, Claude tried to place what country the man might have originated from. Perhaps he had met him in some out-of-the way place back in the years when Europe had been gripped by war and revolution. Dark clothes spoke to him of dark places. The Balkans, perhaps?

He thought of those beautiful cities where east met west, where western propriety met the sensuality of the Orient.

Beautiful memories came to him, memories scented with sandalwood and filled with the sound of rustling silks and tinkling bells dangling from slim wrists and ankles.

Their complexions had ranged from snowy white to deepest ebony. Being a man of science, he had been captivated by the variations there were in and between various races. Small breasts with large pink nipples and thick blue veins were usually found on the snow white girls. Their pubes varied from cotton wool whiteness to deep auburn. Their legs had been slim. Their bottoms as round and pert as that of a young boy.

Discerning as he was, he had never had any favourites among those women. Just as he had enjoyed the pure white, he had also enjoyed the yellow, the cream, the brown and the deep ebony. The latter were especially memorable. One in particular sprang to mind. Her body had indeed bordered on black, but gleamed with the blueness of a sky touched by the first quarter of the moon. Her breasts had been pendulous and had rested on her bulbous belly which in turn had rested on her enormous thighs. A fleece of black wool had spilled from between her mountainous flesh. It had seemed to him at the time as though she were keeping some animal trapped there, the spill of woolly hair being merely its head attempting to surface for air.

The time had come when he had felt like a trapped animal himself. He remembered her torturing him with her gargantuan flesh, wrapping her breasts around his head, his nose against her sternum so he could hardly breathe, and when he did, he breathed her; her hot femininity covering him like a sodden, steamy cloth. Even now, he could recall her smell with the greatest of ease. After all these years, it still made him feel weak, and yet to think of the experience was always satisfying.

Not content with trying to suffocate him with her breasts, she had held his head between her legs which she crossed at the knees like a pair of giant scissors. Her belly had rested on his head and her public hair had muffled his struggling breath.

There had been no doubting what she wanted him to do, and in so doing, Claude had been amazed. He had felt the demand in her clitoris even before seeing it. Wet and fleshy, it had pressed against his chin, pulsing and dancing over his face. Never had he known a woman whose clitoris pushed out and into his mouth like some masculine penis. Never had he beheld such purplish, moist flesh, her inner labia hanging like frills of giant fungus that slapped against his chin.

Like an earthquake, she had rumbled over his face, her climax as shattering as a volcanic eruption, her lava spewing over his chin and trickling down his neck and his chest.

What wonderful days, he thought to himself. Days, unfortunately, that are passed.

He took a quick rest from the telescope and picked up the small notebook in which he wrote his nightly observations; both of humanity and the stars. He passed it to his left hand so it would be there the moment he needed it. He also picked up a pencil which he wound absent-mindedly between his fingers.

With a great deal of mental control, he banished his memories back into his subconscious. There was a time and place for everything, he believed, and at this moment in time he had other things to deal with. The main object of his interest was still the man on the quay. He had now turned and was looking out to sea again.

The man was now doing something that made Claude even more intrigued than he had been. A pair of binoculars were now trained on the outgoing yacht.

Now why would he be doing that? Claude posed himself the question and also attempted to answer it. Of course there were a number of reasons. He liked the sea. He liked boats. Perhaps he was one of those peculiar people who still believed in sea monsters like the one that was said to inhabit a Scottish loch. Was this man purely a voyeur who had stumbled on a lucky coincidence? Yet Claude detected a smile of self-satisfaction. Had this man known what was to happen?

Other people blocked his vision for a moment as they passed between the man and Claude's telescope. There were a few people promenading at this time of night, mostly couples, laughing and chattering excitedly as they made their way back to their hotels, their yachts or their private apartments.

The man came into view again. The binoculars were now hanging from his neck. He was lighting up a cigarette. Claude saw the smoke curl up before his face, saw the self-satisfaction more clearly now.

'A set-up, as the Americans say,' Claude whispered to himself. 'I wonder what you are up to?'

As the man turned to a certain angle, the light from the new street lamp accentuated his features.

Claude stiffened as the light caught a silver streak down the man's right cheek.

'Stavorsky,' he muttered. A sharp crack told him he had broken the pencil.

Chapter 10

Hans van der Loste had a regular mistress whose name was Tanya. She was an attractive girl with coffee cream skin, inky black eyebrows, and lips that looked as though they had been dyed with rose juice.

They were lying in the state room of his motor yacht, *Cartouche*, where a circular bed piled high with cushions took pride of place. The walls were of a honey coloured panelling, and the sheets on the bed were of tangerine coloured silk.

Hans was lying with one arm thrown up above his head. Tanya was beside him, her catlike eyes narrowing as her body undulated against him.

'You seem distracted tonight, my darling,' she murmured in her deeply accented voice. 'Is something troubling you?'

As she asked the question, her fingers divided his sprinkling of golden chest hair, her fingernails lightly scratching his skin. She nuzzled her face against his armpit and gently nipped at the nipple nearest her.

He took a deep, almost regretful breath before he answered. 'Not really.' It was only a half-lie. He had seen the slender blonde girl go aboard the yacht *Stanza* which was moored next to his and owned by a wealthy American named Joseph Michael Carey III, a man he had met before in Vienna or some such place. Normally, the fact that a man was merely wealthy would not have troubled him. But this man had got to the girl before he had. Competition was something he had to contend with in both his business and personal life, but he was never a graceful loser.

But Tanya was here. No doubt, as late evening moved into early morning, Tanya would help him forget that he was harbouring lustful feelings towards the young lady.

No point in dwelling on what might have been or what might

be. A need to be occupied suddenly overcame him. Turning onto his side, he faced Tanya then kissed her forehead.

'Put on those things I bought you in Marseilles,' he murmured, his chill-blue eyes burning into hers.

She smiled her catlike smile, her eyes seeming to match the upward turn of her dark, pink lips.

'If you like,' she purred, and her voice really did seem to resemble that of a cat.

He watched the movement of her wide, expressive behind as she walked away from the bed. Was that the right word? Expressive? He decided it was. Her big, pear-shaped buttocks moved with her walk. It was as if they kissed and caressed each other with every step. Full, womanly flesh that begged to be spanked, gripped or divided by the stiffness of his prick.

When she returned she was wearing the white lace basque he had bought her. Generous as the cup size was, her full breasts appeared balanced on the stiff under-wiring, the pinkness of her nipples peering over the top of an edging of crisp lace.

Tight and extremely complimentary to her narrow waist, the basque ended just below her navel. Strips of fine elastic crossed the creamy expanse of her fleshy thighs before connecting with a pair of extremely ornate lace stockings.

'It's very restrictive, darling,' she said, her hands resting on her hips as she pouted and shrugged her shoulders. Her pout turned to a knowing smile. Intending her expression to be seductive, she raised one eyebrow. 'But you know how I like restriction, darling.'

A thin smile appeared on Hans' lips as he stretched and rested his head on his hands. The area of sheet that covered his hips began to rise with his penis.

'Bend over, darling. Let me see your big, beautiful behind.'

Her teeth flashed big and white as she laughed. After stretching her arms to either side of her, she turned round, opened her legs slightly, and bent over so that her big, beautiful backside was pointing in his direction.

Hans felt his penis make more of an impression in the

sheet. He did not look at it. His attention was fixed on those beautiful, big cheeks and the strange vulnerability of a quim completely devoid of pubic hair.

If her pubic hair had been profuse, he would never have discerned the dark purple opening of her sex and the slippery pinkness of her labia. As it was, he could see every detail of the glistening flesh that sheltered within her fleshy lips. In time he would enter her moist portal. But for now he was content to look at her and contemplate what the blonde girl had done with the American. Then he thought of what he would like to do with the girl in the blue dress.

Tanya began to wriggle her bottom.

'How do you want it?' she asked him.

'Turn round,' he said. 'Let me see your tits over the end of the bed.'

This was not the first time Tanya had been in the master cabin of his yacht, and with any luck, it wouldn't be the last.

Enthusiastic as she was, she lost no time in turning round. She bent forward and gripped each of the bottom corners of the bed. Her breasts, too large and too strong to be restricted by a brassiere of lace, spilled over and hung just above his feet like a couple of ripe melons.

'They look good,' he murmured and was glad that Tanya had pinned her hair high on her head. No shingle for her. And no long hair falling over her body to hide her delights. Tanya was a woman of the old school, delightfully submissive to anything he desired.

Naked, he got up and walked to the foot of his bed. He reached for her breasts, weighed them in his hands, then with a scissor-like motion, he clamped each of her nipples between two fingers.

Eyes wide, breath racing between her parted lips, she stared at him. There was pleading in her eyes, yet she asked no quarter. She groaned, her bottom wriggling to coincide with her heightened desire.

Tanya knew better than to move. She knew what sort of sex

he liked, knew there were other things he would do before he put his prick into her.

Hans ran his hand down over the lace of her basque and onto her big, broad buttocks.

He stood back from them; looked as if deciding exactly what he thought of them or what he intended doing to them. Delightful as the blonde had been, he still had a yearning to divide the big behind he had come to know so well.

But first, a little diversion.

How naked a bottom looks when above is the lace of a basque, he thought, and below is the lace of a woman's stockings. As he thought these profound thoughts, he pulled one voluptuous cheek away from the other. Tanya remained still as he studied the puckered orifice that lay between.

Oh yes, it was something they had done many times before. Many, many times.

Suddenly, he let go of Tanya's behind.

'Lie on the bed,' he said, his voice full of urgency. 'I want to fuck you.'

Tanya looked over her shoulder before obeying.

'Are you sure?' she asked, frowning at this unusual deviation from the norm. 'You don't usually . . .'

There was the sound of a hard slap as Hans' palm smacked hard against one buttock.

'Do as I say!'

Tanya pushed her luck. 'But you don't usually . . .'

Just as she had hoped, her questioning his authority led to another smack. Yet she sensed that the night could end there if she pushed her luck any further. And she didn't want it to end. She enjoyed her trysts with this man, and she made good use of the money he paid her. She intended to get a qualification in beauty therapy. There was money to be had on the Côte d'Azure from old ladies with wrinkles and bodies still aching to be fucked.

Still wondering what had brought about this sudden change in routine, she laid herself out on the bed.

To her surprise, he suddenly leaned against the wall and turned out the lights.

'Don't . . .'

She had been about to say, 'Don't you want to look at me,' but the answer came to her anyway. He didn't want to look at her. It wasn't her into whom he was easing his erection. He was fantasising, imagining it was someone else.

Who, I wonder? But her vagina was filled with him. Involuntarily, her hips began to meet his thrusts. His hands gripped her breasts as though he were trying to make them small enough to fit into his palms. Fat chance! She had big breasts and was proud of them.

'Hans,' she moaned before her sounds of pleasure were silenced by his mouth.

Hans did not want to speak. To speak might shatter the image that was in his mind. In his mind it was the blonde girl beneath him with her small breasts and boyish hips. He thrust at her hard as though he were punishing her for making it with the American. He was sure she had.

Harder and harder, faster and faster he penetrated her, thudded against her. Even though he heard her crying out that his assault was too fierce, too much for her to cope with, he knew she was lying, knew she was enjoying it.

With a tingling and a tremendous sense of relief, he reached the zenith of his excitement, the ultimate moment when sheer energy propelled his fluid out of him and into her.

As the last pulsating moment ebbed away, she cried out. Her hips rose from the bed. He grabbed hold of the large, fleshy bottom he knew so well and held her tight against him until her moment had come and gone.

Satiated with sex, Hans rested his head on his hand and closed his eyes.

'What are you thinking about?' Tanya asked him.

Hans smiled. 'Sex. Don't I always think about sex when I am with you?'

She laughed and rubbed her chin against his shoulder.

'I wouldn't want you to think about anything else. Tell me what fantasy is going on in your head?'

Without opening his eyes, he smiled.

'I was thinking that we have not had a guest in our bed in quite a while.'

Tanya curled herself up against him. Her fingers caressed his chest.

'Not since that North African. The one with the shiny skin and no hair. He was certainly a very big man.'

Hans opened one eye and looked at her. 'You mean he had a very big cock.'

Tanya's laugh was more throaty than before. 'He was very well endowed. But that isn't really what I meant. He was a very big man. Big shoulders. Big chest. Big legs. And that shiny head. I liked the feel of it between my legs.'

Hans turned to face her. He covered one breast with his hand and gently squeezed.

'So you would like to do it again.'

Although she winced as he pinched her nipple, she thrust her belly against him. 'Oh, yes. There is nothing so delightful as having one man behind me and one in front – no matter what the position.'

Hans used her breast to pull her to him. His mouth came close to hers.

'Who said I was talking about another man?'

Tanya opened her eyes wide. 'Weren't you?'

Hans smiled. 'Look at it from my point of view. Two men were good. You said so. Two women will be good. I say so.'

Tanya paused for barely a moment. Then her tongue licked her lips.

'Let's do both,' she murmured, thrusting herself more tightly against him. 'Do you have anyone in mind?'

Hans smiled, then rolled away from her and rested his head on his arm again.

'I think so,' he said softly.

Chapter 11

By morning, *Stanza*, the three-masted schooner belonging to Joseph Michael Carey III, was moored in a small bay just a few miles along the coast from St Asaph.

They awoke still warm with the smell of sex, a patina of sweat covering their skin.

'How about a swim?' suggested Joe.

Mariella looked at him quizzically, a half-smile playing round her mouth.

'I haven't brought a costume with me. Will the natives take fright if they see me going naked?'

Joe only laughed.

Sunrise wasn't long past, but already the breeze was warm.

Joe spread his arms as he showed her the place in which they were anchored.

'See. Not a native in sight. Not even a mud hut.'

'It's a beautiful spot. Better than a bathtub any day,' Mariella responded.

She meant what she said. Nature had indeed provided a sheltered cove where the water was clear and the sand white on the sea bed. Enclosing the beach, lemon-tinted cliffs gleamed in the sunlight.

'Race you!'

They said it in unison, and naked, they dived into the blue water, its coldness taking their breath away.

Sand spilling between toes, Mariella ran up the beach, shaking the water from her hair as she went.

Laughing, her breasts heaving, she threw herself onto the sand which was warm against her back. Joe threw himself beside her.

'I want to make love to you again.' He was leaning across her, his lips just inches from hers.

Mariella closed her eyes and raised her arms above her head.

'You're insatiable.'

'Am I?'

He sounded surprised.

She opened her eyes. It had occurred to her to float off into her fantasy land in order to get the best out of her sex with him, but something held her back. After all, she was here to find something out, not just to enjoy a temporary affair.

She stroked his face and felt the beginnings of stubble.

'How did you become rich, Joe?'

The smile disappeared from Joe's face.

'Why do you want to know?'

She shrugged. 'No real reason. It's just a general question. You don't have to answer it.'

Joe shook his head. 'I'd prefer not to.'

'But you're glad you are?'

A questioning look came to his eyes. 'That's a strange question.'

Mariella pouted. 'I don't see that. All I'm asking is, do you like the fruits of your wealth? I mean, surely it's given you many opportunities. Take travel, for instance. If you didn't have any money, you couldn't travel like you do. Have you been to many places?'

Joe's expression lightened. 'Sure. All over the place. Brazil, Australia, Singapore, Ceylon; you name it, I've been there.'

'And Europe?'

He nodded. 'Every country in Europe. Any you could name.'

'Austria? Hungary? Turkey?'

Smiling, he tapped at her nose. 'Silly goose. Turkey's in Asia. But I have been to Austria and Hungary.'

'When was that?'

For a moment, she thought he wasn't going to say. A haunted look passed over his face before he found the words to tell her.

'About four years ago. I stayed a while in Austria, but not

in Hungary. There were too many things going on in those days. Russia was in uproar and thousands were fleeing over the border – mostly aristocrats.'

'Frightened people,' she whispered, a certain crispness to her voice.

There was a sadness in his eyes. 'Yes. Very frightened people. They'd pay anything to get away. Anything.'

His voice trailed away and there was a faraway look in his eyes. 'Anything,' he repeated.

Mariella judged that talking was at an end. His penis was warm and hard against her thigh. The sand was cooler now against her back, but the sun was getting hotter.

'Kiss me,' she murmured.

His lips closed in on hers, the gap narrowing until flesh met flesh.

In those two, small words, she had asked for more than just a kiss. The beach was deserted, they were naked, and the earth smelt sweet.

They made love on the beach, droplets of water mingling as their bodies met, sand clinging to their skin as they rolled and murmured their passion.

Joe could not know that behind Mariella's closed eyelids, she was seeing her sheik, personified by the enigmatic Valentino. But would Joe care that her mind had substituted a Hollywood movie star for him?

It didn't matter. Mariella would never tell him.

In her mind, she submitted to the man in the dark robes, the man who she continually used in her sexual fantasies.

In reality, she pressed her head into the sand of a deserted cove somewhere along the Côte d'Azure. Suspended again between fantasy and reality, she arched her back away from the beach, and when she came, it was shattering; as shattering as waves crashing on rocks, then gentle, a sinking feeling as the waves receded.

When she opened her eyes, Joe was staring at her. He was blinking and there was an anxious look in his eyes.

'Will I see you again?' His voice sounded brave, but the fear of rejection was in his eyes.

Smiling, Mariella flicked at his wet hair which sent droplets of water trickling down his face to drop off his nose and his chin.

'You may have to tempt me.' Seduction laced her words. Her voice was little more than the murmuring of the surf cascading to the shore. Her body undulated against him. Her tongue licked the salt water from his chin and sucked it from the tip of his nose.

Closing his eyes, he sighed and threw back his head. His chest heaved in another, stronger sigh before he again looked into her face.

'Come to Marseilles with me.'

'To Marseilles?'

He nodded and more water fell onto his face. 'You'll like Marseilles. I'm going there on Friday. I have business there.'

Mariella thought quickly as she stroked his face. She was thinking of how good-looking he was and how pleasant it would be to spend some time in Marseilles; shopping, theatre, dining out – and all at the expense of Joseph Michael Carey III. She suddenly thought of Peter, the dark, surly man who had set her a task. Thoughts of enjoying herself in Marseilles did not vanish altogether, but they did become a little subdued. But Joe would not know of this.

She pursed her lips like a petulant child and kissed his chin. 'Business is boring, darling. How will I occupy myself while you deal with your business?'

The boyish look covered his face as he laughed, creases appearing around his eyes, and his teeth were very white as he threw back his head.

He held her face in his hands. 'Darling,' he said, his voice a little more serious. 'Come with me. I'm sure you'll find the business I have to attend to very interesting. I have many valuable items, you see. Too many to accommodate in my villa in France or my apartment in Detroit. So I'm disposing of a few valuable items.'

Little did he know, but Joe had said exactly the right words to influence Mariella's decision.

'What sort of items?' She said it casually, but her brain was working like the cogs in a clockwork train. This could be the opening she needed – and so soon.

'Pictures and things. Beautiful things. I keep them in a vault at a museum I set up in my mother's name. But there's not room to exhibit them all – not even in the museum. Tell you what,' he said, a look of triumph signalling that he had thought of something truly useful. 'You can choose which things I should sell. How do you like that?'

How did she like it? It was marvellous, though of course she couldn't say that.

'I like it fine,' she responded, hardly daring to believe he was unknowingly making her task that much easier. She hugged him then and ran her hands down to that lovely, male curve between strong back and firm buttocks. 'Your museum isn't too boring, is it?'

His blue eyes sparkled as he shook his head. 'How can it be boring with you there?'

Her look was seductive. 'You think I can improve it?'

He hugged her tight, and as he did so, she felt his penis harden against her belly.

'I'm pretty sure you can, baby. Pretty damn sure!'

Chapter 12

Mariella was feeling pretty pleased with herself by the time she got back to the hotel. She took a deep breath as she collected her key from reception and exchanged a smile with the concierge, whose hair was thin on his scalp but still dark and sleek at the sides. Their fingers touched, lingered a while. A glimmer of something more than mere courtesy was in his eyes.

'Thank you.' She took the key and crossed to where the lifts and the stairs were situated.

As she passed a gilt mirror, she smoothed her hair, then reapplied her lipstick. Her heart began to beat faster. She wanted to be perfect for Peter. She wanted to be exactly as he liked her. The face that looked back at her had eyes that glittered, cheeks flushed pink. Everything a man could want. Unbidden, a shadow crossed her countenance and a more wild look came to her eyes. At the same time a small voice echoed deep inside her head. But why, it asked? He does not own you. She shook her shingled hair so that the light caught it, highlighting more shades than one. Whether it was truth or not, the thought was swallowed. As instructed, she went to Peter's room before going to her own.

Her steps slowed and her heart beat faster the nearer she got to his door.

He was waiting for her, arms crossed and a deep, brooding look beneath his dark brows.

Mariella breezed into the room.

'I'm back!'

Her smile was like that of a child keen to please, but fearful lest she offend.

Through the smoke that seemed permanently to circle his

head, she took note of the dark eyebrows that formed a deep vee above his nose. There was a look in his eyes that was almost accusing.

Although she told herself it was wrong and that she should be ashamed, she could not help but shudder with excited apprehension. Peter always had affected her like that. He was her lover, her master, her Svengali. She was his possession, a sensual instrument that danced to his tune, a tool that helped to shape and fashion his achievements. When she was with Peter, her fantasies were less vivid.

Today his upper body was bare. He wore only a pair of black satin trousers that clung like the skin of a snake to his hips and his legs. Dark hair curled over his chest but did not hide the fact that his muscles were well defined.

Mariella stood before him, her hands clasping her clutch bag a little too tightly, her eyes viewing him a little too fearfully.

'How did you do?' he asked her.

She paused. What mood would best suit him? She decided to be light-hearted.

'Sexually, or otherwise?'

Her smile was bright but it gradually faded once he was towering over her. There was menace in his eyes. She winced as his fingers dug into her arms. Her shoulders hunched up to somewhere near her ears.

'Is that all you have done? Enjoyed yourself?' His voice sounded like sifted gravel rumbling over stone.

Why do you put up with this? asked a voice from deep inside as she squirmed and tried to lean away from him.

He's dark, came the reply. He dresses in black and he dominates.

She made an effort to ignore the fingernails that dug into her flesh. After all, she had achieved something for him. He should be grateful for that. Fear turned to defiance.

'Peter! You did say you wanted me to get close enough to find out whether he has your precious icon. And I may very well have achieved something. He wants me to go to Marseilles with him.'

'So?' He shook her as though shaking the truth out of her like salt from a pot.

'He has a museum there. His mother set it up. It's where he keeps a lot of pictures and things. He's decided to sell some of them and has asked me to choose which things he should sell.'

Peter's grip lessened.

'To Marseilles?' His frown lightened, but there was a new intensity in his eyes. It was as if he had found a pearl inside a shell – and she was only the shell.

She nodded, her mouth hanging open as if she were a fish out of water. At the same time she asked herself why she let him use her as he did. The answer was muted, unintelligible. Despite the scar, he looked like her fantasy lover. He even acted like him.

So do you need the real thing? There it was. A small seed of defiance that given time could grow into outright rebellion. But not yet. She still needed Peter. He was like an opiate she had to have. He would continue to be indispensable until another more beguiling option came along, one who looked even more like her Hollywood idol.

'You will go, of course,' said Peter. A self-satisfied smile spread slowly across his face. Even the deep hollows beneath his cheekbones disappeared momentarily.

His breathing became more noticeable as one hand unfurled from her arm. He ran his fingers through her hair, his breath sounding like a brush sweeping over stone. His chest heaved and she felt herself go weak. As his body came closer to hers, she could feel its heat even before she touched him.

Now there was lust in his smile. Intent in his eyes.

Desire swept through Mariella's body. Like an unseen phantom, nothing more than a dark, creeping shadow, it shivered over her flesh, cramped her belly muscles, and nestled, hot and heavy between her legs.

His arms enveloped her. He hugged her close now, his chin resting on her head as his fingers caressed her hair.

'You did well, my little babushka. Very well indeed. Now you can tell me exactly what you did to him and what he did to you. I want to know everything. Everything.' His voice seemed to melt into softness, and yet its resonance echoed around her head as if there were room for nothing else in her mind.

Words, details and emotion poured out of her. It was as if she were a pomegranate and he were prying out the seeds with a sharp pin. Or Peter was a hummingbird, sucking from a helpless flower. She told him everything about what she had done with Joe Carey. But she told him nothing of what she had done in her mind with the sheik. She never had.

Peter's eyes bored into her once she'd finished.

One look, she thought, and I am heaving with desire.

The silence broke. 'He was that good, was he?' Peter's words were measured though casual.

Mariella thought of the firm young body of the American. Smooth skin against hers. Youthful muscles. The vigour of a man who could finish and then immediately start afresh was impressive. How could it be otherwise?

'Oh yes,' she murmured, emotion born of memory overriding caution. 'He was very good.'

'You bitch!'

Wide-eyed and taken off guard by his exclamation, Mariella attempted to speak.

'What do you . . . ?'

'Silence!'

His expression made her tremble. Because she could not ask him what was the matter, she asked herself. Then it came to her.

'I didn't mean . . .' she began.

'Silence!' he shouted again.

His mood had changed.

Mariella's tongue seemed to curl back into her mouth.

Peter's teeth were clenched and his eyes were pools of vengeful darkness.

'You really enjoyed doing it out in the fresh air, didn't you? Didn't you, you bitch!'

There was no mistaking the underlying excitement beneath his growling voice. Mariella realised that without intending to, she had provided him with an excuse for retribution. But wasn't that always the way with him? Wasn't it as if he were probing into her mind with the intention of having her say something he would not like?

Tingles of expectation raced through Mariella's body. This had happened before. She knew what was to come. Some depraved, erotic scene would be fermenting in his mind. She proclaimed fear, though she felt only excitement. She was impatient to know what he had in store for her.

'Out there,' he said suddenly. He jerked his head in the direction of the balcony. The door was open and white curtains were billowing in with the breeze.

As his hands released her, her arms dropped to her side. She took only two slow steps, her eyes flickering as she watched him choose a long black cord, one of his favourite items.

Her heart began to thump and her breasts swung as she walked in front of him out onto the balcony. She rested her hands on the cold metal of the balustrade and looked out over the city. The sun had set and the lights that lit the quay were throwing their gleam out onto the water.

'Don't turn round,' he ordered. 'Just spread your arms out to either side of you.'

She did so, and although she thought she had spread them enough, he obviously did not.

She gasped as his palm pressed on her back so that her arms spread further and her breasts hung over the metal rail.

If there had been buildings in front of them there was no doubt in her mind that someone would have seen her. But there was only the sea ahead of her. Below her there were only laughing revellers strolling before or after dinner. All were too wrapped up in themselves to look up at the hotel and see her. And even if they did, so what? She wasn't naked, was she?

With her hair tumbling either side of her face, Mariella kept her gaze fixed on the pavement far below. Her breathing became deeper, its pace increasing as the bonds bit into her wrists.

'If you enjoy fresh air so much, then fresh air you will have.'

She sensed the cruelty in his voice and also the excitement. It was said in the sort of way to make him irresistible to her. Having sex with the American had been great. She had enjoyed his affection and his strange belief that she had been a virgin before his violation.

Violation! How could it be called that? His lovemaking had been warm, spontaneous and eminently enjoyable. But it certainly wasn't the same as having sex with Peter.

Peter was dark, and not just in looks. Not knowing what he would do to her next was an adventure. Each time he surprised her, and surprise ultimately led to a greater thrill and volcanic climax.

The turmoil that had started as a seed, grew and reared up again. Why am I like this? she asked herself. I tremble and yet I want him to do these things to me.

Her pulse seemed to pound in her ears and she was having difficulty keeping her breathing steady. She was almost disgusted with herself for letting him tie her hands to the ironwork. Sexual images were flashing on and off in her mind, ignited by what he was doing. It was almost as if she were outside herself, seeing what he was seeing, indeed, playing a part in his intentions.

She gasped as he rolled her skirt up over her back until it rested on her shoulder blades. There was a tearing sound as he ripped her silken underwear away from her body. Now her bottom was bare and she was seeing it through his eyes. Because of that, a wet secretion oozed from her vagina as her muscles contracted. She wanted him to want her even more than she wanted him. If his ways were dark, then so be it.

'This is how you should be,' she heard him say. 'I only want to expose that part of your body that I will use.'

The way she responded to him still surprised her. She felt no revulsion so far, only a thirst for adventure. It was as if she were lined with buttons and he knew exactly which one to press in order to get a response.

Tendons in her neck became taut. She gasped as his hands parted the soft swell of her buttocks. His fingers opened her sex, then entered. She moaned as they probed deeper, her juices squelching like warm honey and making their entry that much easier.

And he would be feeling her warmth, feeling her moist flesh and the seeping liquid running down over his fingers. Eyes half closed, she licked her lips. It was almost as if she wanted to taste herself, or wanted to tempt him into tasting her.

'Take me,' she moaned, her bare bottom wriggling above her firm white thighs and the silky pinkness of her garters. 'Put your cock into me.'

'Is that what you want?' His voice was a low, mocking growl. He pushed his fingers into her with enough force to make her cry out. 'Is that all you want? Just my fingers? Because that is all you are going to get!'

'Yes,' she cried. The word was like a long drawn out hiss. She closed her eyes and behind them felt a burning shame. Her face was pink with exhilaration at the thought of what he might do to her next.

'You are a liar!' he cried.

Her vagina made a sucking sound as he withdrew his fingers.

Her cry was like that of a child from whom the breast has been taken.

'Peter!'

She felt a warm stickiness against her face. She saw his glistening fingers, and as she breathed, she smelt herself on them. Slowly, his fingertips travelled down over her cheeks and left wetness in their wake. She felt shame that her face was smeared with her own juices.

She trembled. She whined with that odd mixture of fear and want he always aroused in her. Let me go, one half of her cried, while the other half begged, Let me stay. Let me be all things to you. Let me be with you.

Her legs trembled as the tip of his penis nudged between the cheeks of her bottom, but ignored her tightest orifice and went on to enter her vagina.

She cried out, the sound hanging in the night air like a late bird.

His penis was filling her, driving against her muscles that gripped him yet also tried to repulse him.

'Now, bitch,' he growled. 'Say how good your American was. Say it!'

The truth of how good Joe had felt was strong in her mind, so strong that she couldn't help exclaiming the truth.

'He was good! I liked the feel of him. I liked it!'

A hand slapped her bottom and left a warm tingling in its wake. It was not unpleasant.

'You're like a bitch! A dog on heat!'

It didn't matter that Peter intended his words to insult, even injure her. Oddly enough, whatever he might call her seemed only to egg her on, to egg him on into becoming more angry and even more jealous.

Deep down, she knew this was true. She knew he became more aroused by her telling him how good another man had been. Just as she knew that his anger only added fuel to the fire of her own desires. She wanted him to respond. She wanted him to punish her for being such a whore, such a slut for enjoying the body of another man, a man who, in effect, he had chosen for her.

Driven by anger, his hands pulled fiercely at her lace camisole that she wore beneath her lovely yellow dress. The fragile fabric gave as his fingers tore into it. Soon, what clothes she wore only covered her shoulders. He had exposed her breasts so that her nipples became purple in the night air. They dangled over the rail of the balcony like juicy grapes.

'I'll show you who's best! I'll show you!' he exclaimed.

His words made her tremble even before his hands gripped her hips. She gave a little cry of surprise as he lifted her and her feet left the floor. Automatically, she bent her knees as he raised her body to meet his. Tense with perverted excitement, she gripped the balcony railing which supported her just below her breasts. The metal dug into her ribs. It was uncomfortable, but not unbearable.

Her body became parallel with the view below. Her ankles met and crossed over behind his back. His rod met no barrier. On the contrary, the slick linings of her inner flesh gushed all over him, drawing him, sucking him deeper and deeper into her body.

She opened her eyes and saw people passing below. Few looked up. Those that did saw only a face looking down at them. They only glanced. It would have taken a longer look to discern that her breasts were hanging over the balcony, swinging in time with an unheard tune. Arms outstretched, it would look as though she were flying.

In a way she was. The more Peter rammed himself into her, the more her breasts swung in the cool evening air, and the more her stomach muscles clenched and pulled him in.

Yet her flying was higher than the hotel they were staying in. Sensations intensified and flitted across her skin, flowed like molten lava through her body. Tendrils of it reached into every part of her. She soared higher, and as she felt him tense, felt his body clamp against hers, she reached the peak of her climax, closed her eyes, held her breath, and although her mouth was open, no sound came out.

His hands stroked her back as he slid out of her. She wriggled against her bonds, inviting him to untie her, but not necessarily expecting it. Peter liked to keep her guessing.

He slapped her bottom. 'I'm going to leave you like that

for a while, my darling. It might help cool you down.' He laughed then and walked away from her.

'Peter! You can't do that! Please! Untie me! Please!'

Her words were wasted. She heard the door close. She was on the balcony entirely alone. What a state to be in! Half – well – almost naked and out on a balcony above the main promenade at St Asaph. And this was all due to Peter. Peter who she had been with for some years. Peter who was dark and mysterious and totally dominating.

In order to pass the time, she attempted to drift into one of her fantasies where Valentino was her lover; dark, dominating, but easy to manipulate.

For some reason, he didn't want to appear. She tried a couple of other costume scenes from some other films he'd starred in.

Nothing happened.

How about Douglas Fairbanks?

But Fairbanks wasn't Valentino. Much as she tried, the fantasy would not form. Peter had left her bereft of sexual appetite. He'd also left her exposed to public view and she had allowed him to do it.

How had this begun, she asked herself? She closed her eyes. Not to lock him out or to try to reclaim one of her sexual fantasies. But just to remember. Just to recall that first time in order to savour it all over again.

Her father had been military attaché at the British Embassy in Vienna at a time when the city was full of refugees. Some were people whose lives had been affected by the Great War. Others were White Russians, aristocrats who had fled Russia with their lives but not necessarily their wealth.

Rather than send her to a finishing school in Switzerland, Mariella's parents had insisted she stay in Vienna. They found a suitable establishment for young ladies, one that catered mainly for the daughters of foreign diplomats and military personnel.

Most of the time, an embassy car had taken her to the academy. Sometimes she stayed overnight in the long dormitory that had cast-iron beds on either side, sky-light windows, and cold water for washing provided by a brass tap and an ice-white sink.

She had shared a bed with her best friend Maria, an Italian girl of dark looks and fiery temper. It was during this time that she had first set her eyes on Rudolf Valentino playing the sheik.

The rest of the audience and the hybrid smell of disinfectant and chocolate had disappeared as Mariella became mesmerised by what she was seeing on the screen.

Passion created by Hollywood and a man with dark eyes and wearing Arabic clothes became much more than that in Mariella's adolescent imaginings.

And yet that passion was not enough for her. To her mind it seemed to stop just at the point where things were getting interesting.

From then on, her fertile imagination had embellished the story with far more explicit acts than would ever be allowed on the screen.

Fantasies became coupled with sexual curiosity. Hidden by darkness and their bedclothes, Mariella and Maria had shown each other their bodies; had even touched those places that were thought most secret, places that propriety forbid them to talk about openly.

Each would tap the other's nipples, their eyes wide with wonder as their plush softness stiffened beneath their fingertips.

'How delicious,' they had murmured beneath the sheet that provided their secret world, and Mariella had started talking about what she would have liked the sheik to do to her.

Maria had blushed and withdrawn from their sexual games. But following a little persuasion from Mariella, she had relented, inhibition overruled by growing sexuality.

'Do it again,' each had urged, not quite understanding that

the feelings aroused could only be assuaged by toying with another part of their bodies.

Once they had tired of playing with each other's nipples and cupping breasts, they caressed each other's buttocks. Again and again, they ran their hands over the swoop of spine where buttocks rise like hillocks from the back's plateau.

It was a while before they had dared to examine what each had between her legs. The lure of the area never talked about, the sanctuary hidden behind their flowering pubic hair, was too strong to resist.

Crisp curls were twined around virgin fingers. Sexual lips were gently prodded and pinched. With light, fairy strokes, they caressed the silky satin of their inner thighs; delicate touches that made each girl sigh with delight.

Once breached, their sexual lips parted. The forbidden place yielded up its treasures. With youthful curiosity, they went on to discover the delights of the pink button that hid among the slippery flesh.

Of course, it was not long before they also slid tentative fingers into melting vaginas. Thus they discovered the sensation that is at first a mere tingle, then as if one is floating, climbing, stretching high; then the sudden explosion, as if a thousand stars are showering down, sinking earthwards.

Moans of delight accompanied their exploits. Other girls shouted for them to be quiet, told them they should not have eaten so much cheese at bedtime, then they wouldn't be having nightmares. They had giggled at that. How could they admit that they were not having a nightmare, or indeed even a dream, but a beautiful reality.

It was hard, but they did try to control their sounds of pleasure. Youthful desire being what it was, and degree of both arousal and orgasm a haphazard subject, the sounds continued. In time, they were found out.

The mistress of the establishment told them she would not tell their parents.

'I have no wish to upset your parents and to bring shame upon this school. Do you both understand that?'

Maria had muttered that she did.

Mariella had stood silently, her eyes downcast.

Frau Hercle was a lady with broad shoulders and yellow plaits twined in a grim figure of eight style at the back of her head. Her breasts thrust against her yellow striped blouse in flagrant contrast to the small white collar at her throat and the neat white cuffs at her wrists. In a certain light, it looked as though her bosoms were straining against the blouse whilst the collar and cuffs were doing their best to stop them breaking out.

Stern in expression, nose as out of proportion to her face as her bust was to her body, she glared down at them.

'But you will be punished,' she added, and the girls trembled.

Maria began to cry. Mariella bit her lip and studied her shoes through half-closed eyes. She remained standing very straight with her hands clasped tightly behind her back.

You'll be all right, she thought to herself. Pretend you're somewhere else.

In the dark office where the windows had thick glass that blurred the school from the outside world, they were told to let down their knickers and bend across the desk. Then they were told to hold up their dresses so that their youthful, firm little buttocks were exposed, ready to receive the sting of the bunch of dried twigs tied with a pink ribbon. The device was kept specifically for such occasions.

Maria had been birched first and it wasn't long before the tears were flowing more loudly and copiously than before.

Mariella had gritted her teeth and clenched her fists, but kept her eyes wide open as she leaned across the desk. The first kiss of the twigs stung, but she did not cry out. She only gritted her teeth more tightly. There was pain, yet each time the twigs landed on her behind, her hips jerked against the edge of the broad desk which was heavily carved, full of nodules, round protrusions shaped as fruit and longer ones shaped as birds and leaves.

Much as the twigs stung and her bottom warmed, she did not cry out. Instead, only a low moan escaped her lips, the moan intensifying each time the twigs landed and her virgin sex jerked against the wooden carvings.

Defiance melted as the protruding carving caused wonderful sensations to cluster somewhere behind her pubic hair. Her eyes closed. Delightful sensations were clustering around the exact spot where Maria's fingers had worked the most wonderful feelings.

Behind her closed eyelids, Mariella began to drift into the darker corners of her mind. She imagined she was at the pictures; there was a small one in Vienna showing mainly American films. Her favourite was always Rudolf Valentino, sultry star of the silent screen. Her favourite subject had always been the sheik and the 'fate worse than death'.

Now she knew exactly what it meant. Yet it wasn't worse than death. On the contrary, she was thoroughly enjoying it.

Valentino's dark eyes had burned into hers. 'I am going to beat you into submission,' he told her, and she had whimpered with joy.

In her mind, a black eunuch was beating her with the bundle of sticks whilst the sheik looked on, his dark eyes burning, his smile almost mocking.

Soon, there was no sign of a whimper in her moan. Instead, the moan rose, became more expansive, more consistent with what was happening to her.

Aware that something strange was going on, Frau Hercle beat harder, but it did no good. Instead of crying out in pain, Mariella had cried with joy. Without the aid of her friend Maria, but purely of her mind, she had experienced something sweet. Something that would never be forgotten, but also something that would set a pattern for the future. There was only one thing missing. The one thing she had not tried yet. A man!

Chapter 13

Because of a shortage of embassy cars, the day came when Mariella had to walk to the Mildehelm Academy for Young Ladies.

Wearing a pale mauve cloche hat with a purple feather at the side, a matching coat with a grey fur collar, flesh-coloured stockings and purple shoes, she had set off, a matching clutch bag held tightly under her arm.

She tucked her gloved hands under her fur collar, turned it upwards and felt its softness on her face. Her step was brisk. It was not a great distance to the academy, but loitering to admire brightly lit shop windows could easily make her late. But it was hard not to be distracted.

The last leaves were floating from the trees in the fashionable squares. Most of the small cafés that edged the squares and trickled along the pavements had removed their tables and chairs from outside, though a few stalwarts remained, unwilling or unable to believe that winter was definitely coming.

Grubby clouds had sagged overhead. They were ragged, she remembered, as craggy as seaside rocks gathered around places where a blue pool of brightness showed through.

As yet, the weather was bracing rather than bitter. Mariella was not averse to finding her own way to the academy. The city when viewed on foot was far more interesting than from a car window.

To get to the academy, she had to cross the Danube, and in order to cross the Danube, she had to catch the ferry along with many other citizens of the throbbing, ancient city.

As usual, burgers in homburgs, black coats and carrying

sporty walking sticks, jostled with office workers and women off to clean for those who were better off than they.

The ferry was not reserved for pedestrians. Cars lined up with bicycles. There was even a pair of golden Haflingers, their manes plaited with ribbons and pulling a baker's dray.

As the ferry shoved off, Mariella had made her way to the rail, chin supported in her palm, eyes raking the shore but not really noticing anything. The river was grey, swollen by rain and silt from the far off mountains. Now and again a ray of sunlight had broken through. For a moment the greyness of both city and river was relieved. Stone carvings on old buildings became more alive. The river almost turned blue.

Mariella waited for the sunlight to touch her.

Then I too might become more animated, she thought to herself.

She had a yearning for something to happen, something akin to her fantasies. Not that she expected Valentino, the black robes floating out behind him as he galloped through the Viennese squares to snatch her away and subject her to that 'fate worse than death'. So far, unfortunately, her fantasies had not come true.

Nothing much had happened since her chastisement with Maria, except that the gardener at home had showed her his penis. She had not been impressed. It had been long and white. Its tip had reminded her of a closed toadstool. She'd giggled.

'It should be painted red and sprinkled with white dots,' she'd laughed. Her disdain had been noticed by the gardener, but all the same, he had invited her to touch it. Out of curiosity rather than desire, she had reached out, felt the velvety flesh and seen the pallid appendage jerk beneath her touch, grow and stiffen to surprising proportions.

Just when she had been considering whether she should find out what it would feel like inside her, a flow of white stuff had spurted from the end and spilled down the front of her skirt.

'Sorry,' the gardener had said, his voice muted with apology. His face had reddened and there was a look of shame in his eyes. 'If you wait a bit, we can do it properly.'

Shaking her head, she had turned and walked away. The gardener had a nice tool, but he had ginger hair and freckles; not features that appealed to her.

The sort of man who appealed to her came into her dreams at night. Like a brigand, he would take her away with him, be masterful, be almost cruel in his love for her. A childish notion, some would have called it, but slowly her dream lover was taking over her life.

She had told Maria about it after their experience in Frau Hercle's study. But Maria had shrunk from her confession.

'How could you want such a man?' she'd exclaimed, her dark hair bouncing and her eyes dumbly pleading like some cast-off spaniel.

But Maria was not Mariella. Mariella was sure her chance would come, and even though she could not expect the sheik or even Valentino, the man that brought him to life, she was sure she would come across someone similar. On that day she had crossed the Danube when her brigand appeared.

A shadow passed first between her and the shore. Then a man's face came into view. Like the other businessmen, he wore a black hat, but a wider, more expansive type than a homburg. His clothes were completely black. So were his eyes and hair. As sunlight finally struck them both, she noticed a scar down his right cheek. It was not red and livid as some scars are, but shiny; as though the skin was thin in that place and looked like satin. The scar ran from his cheekbone to the corner of his mouth. It gave him a slightly cruel, sardonic look.

He wished her good morning. At first she had been disinclined to speak, like any young lady should. Who was this stranger who had appeared as if from nowhere? His eyes seemed to bore into hers, just like her hearthrob on the silver screen. Her heart was thudding against her ribs.

His smile made her ignore the sardonic twist to his mouth and the scar seemed of no consequence. She had automatically reached up and touched his lips just to test that they were real. That he was real.

Right from the first, Peter had treated her as if he knew her well. And the way he had looked at her on that very first day, completely obliterated any distrust she might have felt. It was as if his eyes were looking into her very soul and her soul belonged to him.

From then on she opted to walk to the academy. Of course, she did not walk all the way. From the ferry onwards, Peter took her in his car. The chauffeur was the only other person in that car, but he was apart from them, divided by a partition of plate glass.

At first they only sat on the warm leather seats, hardly speaking but knowing that each was wondering about the other. It was as if an electrical field was bristling between them.

When they did speak, their conversation was trivial. They asked small questions of each other.

'What does your father do?' he'd asked her.

'Military attaché,' she'd replied.

He'd also asked her when she was likely to be married – not if, when!'

'My father wants me to,' she explained.

'But you don't.'

Their eyes had met.

'No. I want adventure first.'

He had nodded slowly, his eyes smiling in tune with his mouth.

'But you wish to know a man?'

Mariella had tilted her head and raised her eyebrows. 'Know a man? But I know many men.'

Peter had shook his head again. This time he laughed.

'Are you mocking me?' she asked sharply.

Slowly again, he had shaken his head. Everything about him

seemed slow, yet at the same time was deeply methodical, even menacing. He was even slow in his seduction of her.

She did not know it at the time, but Peter was purposeful in such matters. He understood that seduction should be slow if it was to be intense enough to last.

One particular day, Peter laid his hand on the seat between them. Mariella glanced down at it. Suddenly her breast had heaved. Seeing his hand there, his fingers, one sporting a gold ring with a flamboyant crest, she felt more curious about him, more intrigued by what his intentions were.

Steadily, slowly, thoughtfully, her fingers moved across the leather. Her hand covered his. She stroked each of his fingers in turn. They responded to her touch, spreading wide like a woman about to be mounted.

She stared at his hand. An odd tingling sensation was running up her arm and from there, throughout her body.

It was as if something warm was flowing from his hand to hers, permeating her flesh, creeping over her skin like shadows dancing over a meadow.

Transfixed, she kept her eyes fixed on his fingers. Not because she particularly wanted to, but because she was afraid to look up into his face.

This, she thought to herself, is the time. All the nights spent beneath the sheets with Maria had been in preparation for this moment. Soon, at the tender age of seventeen, she would be a virgin no more.

'Please,' she said to him. 'I think I want to make love with you.'

But the moment had to be right, he said to her. Everything had to be satisfactory to both. He asked her about her experiences.

At first she was loath to tell, but his eyes seemed to bore into hers, digging into her brain until the words poured out like loosened earth.

She told him of what she had done with Maria in the dormitory and of how Frau Hercle had punished them.

She detected a sudden sparkle in his eyes when she told him that bit.

'Did you like what she did to you?' he asked.

'Like?' Mariella's breast had heaved as she thought about it. She had even asked herself the same question. Had she liked it, or had she merely been enjoying the fantasy that was happening in her mind.

'I think I did,' she answered at last.

Somehow she did not want to admit to her favourite fantasy. It was hers alone, and never mind how much like a satanic sheik this man might look, she was not going to tell him all her secrets.

There was still the matter of her virginity to be taken. Neither were keen to use the back seat of the car. She had to be at her most relaxed, he had told her. Preferably when she was about to go to sleep.

She told him about her bedroom at home; the servants always on hand, the high window that looked over a garden where stone cherubs peed into baroque fountains. She told him of the honey coloured walls, the thick carpets, the creamy lace curtains at the window and those on her bed.

'Too many servants,' he had said calmly.

She told him about the dormitory at the academy and how they tied her hands at night so she would not play with herself.

Full of sudden fire, his eyes met hers. He said nothing.

He had come to her when she least expected it.

She was staying over at the academy that night, not sharing with Maria this time, but in a bed on her own shielded from the rest of the dormitory by a free-standing screen.

As usual, once she was in bed, Madame Frenais, the French mistress, had pulled back her bedclothes and produced the wrist bands that would tie her hands to the metal rungs above her head. Self abuse, she had been told in a lecture following the application of the bunch of twigs, was a dangerous and sinful pastime. This was the reason why she rarely stayed overnight nowadays. She preferred to go home and pleasure herself in the privacy of her own bedroom. But at present her parents were on a visit to Slovakia. She had been ordered to stay at the academy.

Midnight brought sleep, though not rest. Mariella's sleep had been troubled. Her body had been in need of being touched. She was denied the opportunity to do so.

In her dreams she imagined that Maria was again running her hands over her flesh, her nails scratching slightly. She groaned as the image faded. The picture of a dark-haired, dark-eyed Maria was replaced by Peter. Mariella groaned and arched her back as if she really were offering herself to him.

She tried rubbing her thighs one against the other, but the touch was too delicate, the movement too weak to bring her relief.

Restrained as her hands were, she tossed and turned, arching her back, body undulating, inner thighs rubbing against each other. Her body was hot, boiling, aching to be touched, and yet there was no relief.

She groaned and a tear squeezed out from the corner of one eye. Her groans turned to sobs. This was hell. There was no punishment in being bound in itself. Being denied sexual relief was her true torment.

Just when she felt she would turn to steam, she imagined the bedclothes were pulled down to the foot of the bed. She felt her heavy nightdress being rolled up until it settled above her breasts. The coolness of night caressed her body and sent goose bumps racing over her skin. She murmured with pleasure, and in her dreams she was stretched out naked in a silent desert beneath a midnight sky.

Hands covered her breasts, enveloped them completely before thumbs pressed against her nipples. Hell had turned to heaven. Her dream had become reality.

She gasped and would have moaned out loud, but a mouth covered hers, a tongue snaked between her lips.

'Quiet!' a voice demanded. 'You must be quiet.'

It was only then that she came to full wakefulness.

Her eyes flicked open. She saw Peter, the Russian count she kept seeing on the ferry. She opened her mouth to exclaim.

He put one finger up in front of his lips and bid her be quiet again.

'This will help.' Before she could express what she was feeling, he had forced her nightdress into her mouth. 'Chew on it. Bite on it, but do not cry out. Not if you want me to pleasure you. Not if you want to finally become a woman.'

Wrists still tied above her, mouth gagged with the hem of the thick cotton nightdress, Mariella ached with pleasure. She arched her back, and as she did so, Peter's hands went beneath her, each clasping a round, firm buttock.

When he kissed her breasts, she thought she would swoon.

When his tongue flicked over and around her nipples, she felt she could fly.

When his penis entered her, she was glad she could not cry out.

Her cries of pain, of pleasure, would have brought everyone running. She could not have helped herself.

Now he was doing everything to her that Maria had done, but with one special extra. Maria had not had a penis. On that first night and many that followed, Mariella found out what it was like to have a penis in her vagina, in her mouth or between her buttocks.

Seventeen. Three years ago.

Unashamed, she had run away from home, told them of her liaison with an exiled Russian count.

Embarrassed by their daughter's behaviour, her parents had announced that she had gone abroad to do good works in tropical climes.

No one questioned their declaration too keenly just in case their own family got infected with the missionary bug.

She was twenty now. Peter was still her brigand, the man who loved her and loved to be cruel. The man who had taken her away from a life and a place where sexual relief was a terrible sin.

She found it amusing now to think that her hands had been bound in order to prevent her following one perversion only. That fact had formed the basis of much more sexual experience. Influenced by Peter and the events at the academy, she had become a willing supplicant to whatever he wanted. She had grown older, yet still she fantasised. Peter did not always make her happy, but for now he was Valentino become reality.

Chapter 14

Peter bathed then dressed for dinner. Once neatly attired in the sort of outfit befitting a Russian aristocrat on his way to dine in the restaurant of the best hotel in town, he glanced out onto the balcony where the near-naked Mariella was still bound by her wrists to the balcony railing.

'Goodbye for now,' he called. 'I will see you later.'

He closed the door of his room behind him but not without adding the 'Do Not Disturb' sign to the door. He would take a sinister pleasure in leaving Mariella as she was, but he would not expose her body or her shame to hotel staff. That, he told himself with smug satisfaction, would be too far beneath him. Besides, some surly valet might take advantage of her himself, and then what would he do? It was quite one thing to order her to have sex with men for his own ends or pleasure. But each man she had been ordered to seduce had been of a certain calibre. Even if they did not have titles, they would at least have money. Less than that and they were merely peasants.

Count Peter Stavorsky, to give him his proper name, descended slowly down the curving staircase that led into the hotel reception.

The staircase was broad, its carpet of a deep honey colour, and its banister of polished maple. It was, he told himself, almost as grand as the staircase of his old home back in Russia, though nowhere near as grand as that in the Winter Palace at St Petersburg, or indeed any other of the Tsar's splendid homes at which he had been a guest on many occasions.

As his thoughts went back to Russia, a faraway look came to his eyes. In his mind he had turned back the clock. He was again a handsome young man, his face unmarked by the cruel thrust of a peasant's blade. Pride returned to his eyes and there was a hint of grandeur in the way he descended the staircase. It was almost as though he were striding in time with a marching tune, one only he could hear.

Once he had gained reception, he turned to the left and, still walking with a hint of pomp and circumstance, he made his way to the restaurant.

Just like the rest of the hotel, the restaurant was a pretty grand affair. Vaulted pillars rose upwards, and where there might have been a carved roof expected, or the vivid, energetic stances of painted gods and goddesses, there was instead a vast, glass dome.

Small lights were set on each white-clothed dining table, their glow like a swarm of fireflies dancing in the dark. Minimal light was all that was needed. The dome overhead let in what light was available from outside. Tonight, of course, it let in only star-shine, yet even that seemed enough to provide an atmosphere of intrigue rather than gloom.

A waiter showed him to a table next to a window that overlooked the harbour.

The waiter pulled back his chair then nudged it forward just before his backside landed on the seat. Without a word but with a courteous demeanour, the dark-haired attendant flicked the linen napkin so it gave a crack like the sudden snapping of an exceptionally crisp twig.

'The menu, monsieur?'

As Peter took the menu, something caught his eye.

Somewhat surprised, he looked again and noticed that the waiter was wearing an exceptionally fine ring on one finger.

His nostrils flared then flattened to mere slits as he drew in breath. The emblem engraved on the ring was very familiar. His fingers immediately wound around the man's wrist.

'Where did you get that?' he snarled.

The waiter was still holding a soup spoon he had been about to put down on the table. His fingers tightened around it. When he answered, his voice was surprisingly calm.

'From my family, sir.'

Peter glared at the ring then looked up into the man's face. He tightened his grip on the waiter's wrist. If the man felt increased pain, he gave no sign of it. Peter squeezed harder.

'You are a liar! That is a Russian ring. You are not a Russian.'

'No, sir. I am not. But I can assure you, this ring was handed down to me by my mother.'

Peter's frown deepened as he looked into the waiter's dark eyes. He noted they were almost as dark as his, but not quite. More a warm, dark brown. Like brandy. French brandy.

'Are you French?' Peter asked him.

'Oui, monsieur,' the waiter replied, his voice as calm as his looks.

He eyed the man's broad shoulders. 'Of good peasant stock, I shouldn't wonder.'

A look of amusement seemed to cross the waiter's face, then was gone. Courtesy was maintained. 'Not quite, monsieur.'

Peter looked searchingly into the man's face, his fingers still holding his wrist in a vice-like grip.

Perhaps more would have been said, but another customer at another table curtailed the incident.

'Garçon!' The voice was strident, though not vulgar.

'Sir,' said the waiter, his voice now soft but firm. 'I think I should be about my work. Another guest requires me.'

As politely as before, the waiter nodded and his eyes indicated the man who had called for attention. He was a big man with short blond hair. There was an impatient frown on his face and he was half rising from his chair.

Perceiving the potential violence in the other man's stance, Peter let go of the waiter's arm.

Seeing that he was about to be dealt with, the big blond man sat down. The tawny-haired woman he was with leaned towards him, seeming to whisper something in his ear. Her lips were against the blond man's ear, but her eyes were on Peter.

Peter recognised a woman's interest when he saw it. He also recognised the blond man as Hans van der Loste, the Dutch diamond merchant who owned the motor yacht *Cartouche*.

He raised his glass to both the man and the woman. He smiled. The big Dutchman and his woman reciprocated.

It was no surprise to receive an invitation to join them at their table.

'I would be delighted,' he told the waiter who brought him the message.

Smiling, he got up from the table, adjusted his jacket and straightened his bow tie. There was pride in the way he held his shoulders. Triumph gleamed in his eyes. Count Peter Stavorsky was pleased with himself. Here he was getting close to Van der Loste without the assistance of Mariella, his little sex slave. In fact, he was so pleased with himself that he failed to notice the waiter with the ring had disappeared and another had taken his place.

Chapter 15

Besides feeling decidedly chilly, Mariella was also beginning to feel angry.

Since first meeting Peter, she had gone along with his power games, enjoying them as much as he did – partly because sexual adventure suited her nature and her incessant fantasies about Valentino and the part he had played in one film, partly because he still looked like her movie idol, so she was still enthralled by him, though not quite as much as she used to be. The young girl of seventeen he had snatched from the Viennese Academy was now a young woman of twenty. She had come of age.

She twisted her hands against her bonds, wriggled her body and managed to get her dress to slide back down a little, though it only got as far as her waist.

Her sigh was one of impatience. How long would it be until he returned? Her arms were aching, and so was her neck after being in the same position for so long.

Laughter drifted up from the promenade, and for the first time ever, Mariella found it impossible to retreat into her dream world.

Groups of people linked arm in arm walked by, their step brisk and merry. Off to parties, she supposed, and wished she were going with them.

Up until now her social life had always included Peter. Much as she might have wanted to have her own circle of friends, Peter had dictated who she was to talk to, who she was to get close to. She had a sudden yearning to do something different and to take a taste of reality.

At the moment, it was impossible to do anything. Much as she struggled, she could not free herself from her bonds.

The shadows on the balcony were getting darker. The moon had risen, shedding a stripe of sparkling silver that shivered and danced over the surface of the sea. The yachts in the bay had a ghostly look about them, as though they were not real at all, but playthings of moonshine and shadow.

Mariella sighed and laid her head on one arm. A small tear squeezed out from the corner of her eye. Needful of making time pass more quickly, she dozed.

Valentino, either as the sheik or anyone else, refused to come to mind. But I need you, her mind screamed, but still he did not come.

'I'll do anything you want. Where are you?' she whispered.

Nothing happened.

Instead of her familiar fantasies, she escaped instead to her memories.

Thoughts of Vienna filled her mind; the boulevards, the cafés, the smell of tobacco, thick coffee and rich brandy. The sound of people talking, laughing. The swish of skirts, the tap of canes as people walked by.

So real was her dream, so intent her preoccupation with escaping her present predicament, that she was only vaguely aware that the swishing sound was a reality. A sound like the tapping of a cane, or the footfall of someone moving quickly came to her.

Because she wanted to be elsewhere, she ignored it and stayed with her dreams of Vienna.

At first it seemed that she really was somewhere else. She felt far more comfortable than she had done. Suddenly her bonds were not as tight as they had been. Her muscles were no longer aching.

Was it still her imagination that her elbows were now bent and her head was resting on her arms? That was the way it felt.

Feeling warmer, she sighed. It was as if her dress had dropped around her and she was no longer exposed to the night air. She felt more comfortable.

The Viennese scenes melted away as she slowly regained full wakefulness. She blinked as she opened her eyes and saw the lights of the promenade snaking along the bay. She raised her head and saw the moonlight dancing on the sea. Then she looked down at her hands. They were folded just beneath her chin. Her dress really did cover her body.

A silk scarf fluttered between the railings of the balcony. She watched in amazement as it drifted down to the ground. Another scarf lay near the railings, disturbed by the breeze, but disinclined to join its partner. These, she decided, were the bonds that had tied her.

Feeling relieved but a little confused, Mariella turned towards the glass door that divided the balcony from the room within. As she stretched her arms, her first thought was that Peter had returned. She frowned. Funny that she hadn't heard him. Was it another of his jokes? Had he been meaning to surprise her?

'Peter?' She kept her voice even; not too loud. Her eyes scrutinised the room.

There was no reply, no movement. A bronze table lamp with a shade fashioned from many strips of coloured glass was the only light from inside the room.

The door squeaked as she opened it, the warmth of the room enveloping her like cotton wool, soft and welcoming.

After closing the door behind her, she rubbed at her arms, revelling in the higher temperature. A puzzled frown remained on her face.

'Peter?' She said it louder this time.

There was still no reply. Nothing moved. No one answered. The room was empty.

Perhaps . . . ? she thought.

She walked into the bathroom, smelt the mix of eau de cologne and shaving soap. Only her own reflection looked back at her from of the bathroom mirror. She walked back out again, her eyes continuously searching for whoever had untied her.

A sudden movement caught her eye. The door that led out into the hotel corridor stirred on its hinges. It was open, yet Mariella was sure Peter had shut that door. She had heard it slam, heard the key turning in the lock. Was Peter playing another game? Had he come back to untie her, then gone off again?

Suddenly annoyed, she grabbed for the door handle and looked out into the corridor. Wildly agitated, her gaze followed the brown and green striped carpet, slid over the pale mint walls. Lights shaped like giant sea shells were set into the walls on either side.

The corridor was empty.

She heard a sudden sound; a lift door closing.

'Peter!' She hissed his name through clenched teeth. 'Your games are becoming too much. I don't know that I like them any more!'

Without looking back, she slammed the door behind her and ran towards the lift. For now she would play his little game. She guessed it would be something like hide and seek, and once she had found him, he would reward her with a night of decadent passion. If she did not find him, he might punish her by ignoring her altogether, going to his own room and locking the door against her.

Yet she was still angry with him. For the first time ever, she wanted to confront him; wanted to tell him that her taste for his games was on the wane.

Joe hadn't treated her like that. That's what she'd like to say to him. Joe had been passionate, kind and full of . . . Her thoughts seemed to hang in suspension as she searched for the right word.

'Youth,' she murmured softly, and felt a sudden surge of emotion that was similar to intoxication. Joe had indeed been full of youth. And so innocent. Fancy thinking her a virgin. That was one piece of information she had not given Peter – that and the details of her fantasies. The reason was not clear, but perhaps because it had struck a chord with her it had become precious. Anyway, it was her secret. Her personal secret.

The lift grille and beyond it the dark emptiness of the lift shaft were immediately before her, the cables spinning slightly as the lift went upwards. There was a clock arrangement above the lift on which a big, black arrow pointed to the floor the lift had stopped at.

Tucking her hair behind her ears, Mariella tilted her head back and watched as the arrow climbed from six to seven, seven to eight. The arrow stopped at the figure ten. There it paused. From somewhere high above, Mariella heard the sound of the lift door clattering open. She heard the clattering for a second time as the bellboy tugged at the inner and outer grille to close it again.

She rang the little bell arrangement at the side of the lift, then watched as the arrow descended around the clock face. She rang the bell for a second time, just to make sure that the bellboy had heard her.

The metal diamonds of the lift grille altered shape and pattern as the interior grille appeared behind it. The bell boy, neat in a suit of dark blue with bright brass buttons, was standing to attention.

Immediately the lift stopped, he grabbed hold of the brass handle of the inner door and pulled it back. He did the same then to the outer one.

'Tenth floor, please,' Mariella said.

The bell boy looked askance. He shook his head. 'I can't do that, miss.'

She pursed her lips and clasped her hands in front of her.

'Why ever not?'

The bell boy looked her up and down. 'It's private, miss.'

'What's private?'

'The tenth floor is private, miss.'

Like some village washerwoman, Mariella's hands went to her hips. Didn't Peter know when to stop? She leaned towards the young man so that her nose was none too far from his.

'Has he paid you to say this?'

The young lad frowned. 'Of course he has. He's my employer, miss.'

Mariella frowned. Was she that wrong? 'Who is your employer?'

'Monsieur Doriere, miss. He owns the hotel.'

Mariella straightened up. She sighed. Suddenly she felt a fool.

'You mean Count Stavorsky didn't pay you to . . .'

Her voice trailed away. Disappointed that she had found no one on whom to vent her frustration, she leaned against the lift wall and closed her eyes.

When she opened them, she saw that the young man looked even more puzzled than he had before.

'I'm sorry, miss. But I don't know quite what you mean.'

Mariella shook her head and ran one hand through her hair. She smiled a shy, embarrassing kind of smile.

'I'm sorry. I must have been mistaken.' She felt her face reddening.

What an idiot, she thought to herself. Imagine bursting in on the owner of the hotel, imagining he was Peter.

The bell boy was now tapping the brass handle with impatient fingers.

'What now, miss?'

Mariella hesitated and sighed dejectedly. She took a step over the small gap between lift and corridor. 'Well, I might as well go to my room, order some supper from room service, then go to bed. What else is there to do?'

The bell boy grinned and winked. 'On a night like this, miss? There's a full moon out. The night is young, and any young man in St Asaph is yours for the asking. No need to turn in so early. No need for room service either.' He did a quick take of the empty corridor before reaching into the tiny slit of a pocket on the right side of his jacket.

'Here, miss,' he said.

She took a small card from his fingers.

'Good little café,' he said quickly.

Mariella studied the wording. Café Noir Nuit. Black Night Café.

She thought of what Peter might say and started to hand the card back to him. 'No. I don't think . . .'

Then she stopped. Her hair escaped from behind her ear and swung around her face as she turned her face back towards him.

Where was Peter? Wasn't he out enjoying himself? So why shouldn't she?

Her mind was made up.

'Wait a minute while I get some money from my room.'

Without waiting for his reply, she dashed along to her own room, changed into a fresh outfit and grabbed the small white leather clutch bag she particularly favoured for evenings out.

'Ground floor,' she exclaimed as she got back into the lift. She smoothed her hair flat with her hands. 'I'll take up your recommendation.'

'Good,' he grinned and winked like he had before. 'And I'll take up my ten per cent,' he said in French, assuming she would not understand him.

'Good for you,' Mariella commented in English.

Chapter 16

During the time Mariella had been 'indisposed' on the hotel balcony of her lover's room, Peter had been enjoying himself.

Hans van der Loste did not recognise him from those years ago in the Balkans when Peter had been fleeing the Communist rebels along with many others. But then, of course, he wouldn't. The story Peter had given Mariella about the icon was not strictly true.

Luckily for him, he had sequestered a sizeable chunk of his wealth abroad prior to the revolution. Only the icon had got left behind, its value alone more than quadruple the amounts in his Swiss, New York and London bank accounts.

He had first seen the icon in the small church of St Boris in the village of Skedanya, about one hundred miles between Moscow and the country palace of his family. Once seen, it was something not to be forgotten. The thick gold that formed its frame and its arched doors were encrusted with rubies, emeralds and diamonds, stones of strong colour and phenomenal worth.

That was another little lie he had told Mariella, sweet child as she was. The icon had never belonged to his family. Catherine the Great had bequeathed it to the Russian Orthodox Church shortly before she died. The gift was probably by way of some sort of penance for her sins which were predominantly those of the flesh. It was well known that the woman had a lover of twenty-one when she was pushing seventy.

Perhaps the wily Potemkin, her senior minister and sometime lover, had advised her to placate the church fathers so they would turn a blind eye to her iniquities. And that was why he found the icon irresistible.

It had belonged to Catherine, the scarlet empress whose favoured young men always ended up as Master of Horse, a suitable title for those who were required to perform like prize stallions.

He imagined that if he had been at her court, that she would have bestowed her favours on him. Perhaps, he confided to himself, I might even have become Tsar.

The thought gave him an enormous feeling of excitement, and left him with the impression that if he did indeed obtain the icon, he would become a very powerful man of long lasting sexual potency.

Peter's eyes had rested on the icon each time he had attended church in the company of his family, some of whom were devout, and some merely dutiful.

In fear of his life, he should have left immediately the rebels stormed the Winter Palace, but the thought of the icon, Catherine's icon, falling into their hands was too much to bear. He stole it from the church and would have got clean away with it if it hadn't been for the son of a French seamstress.

'It is not yours. It belongs to the church,' the young man had said.

Peter had merely laughed and knocked the young man to the ground. He had thought he had left him for dead, but to his annoyance, the boy came rushing up to him just as he was about to cross the Trans Siberian Railway line.

This time, it was Peter who came off worse. The knife had been almost hidden in the young man's hand. Peter had been unprepared. There was a stinging pain in his side, then another as the knife had slashed his face. He had fallen to the ground, his blood staining the snow. When he came to, the icon was gone.

There was no time to search for the thief. The rebels were too close. Hiding by night and travelling by day, he had made the border and crossed into the Balkans.

The scar on his face also injured his mind. The icon became

an obsession. From country to country he went, asking questions, seeking appointments with auction houses, banks and other financial institutions that might be able to help.

A dealer in Vienna finally gave him the lead he needed. Another dealer had purchased items for an American woman and a Dutchman. Peter had made further enquiries. The American woman was dead but her son, Joseph Michael Carey III was alive and might now have the icon in his possession. The other man was Hans van der Loste. Coincidentally, it turned out that both kept yachts at the stylish coastal resort of St Asaph, and both were men who loved all things of classic quality, and that included women.

Van der Loste was smiling at him across the blue and red flower arrangement that sat in the middle of the table. His blue eyes almost disappeared as he did so.

'Would you do me the honour of having a night cap with me, Count Stavorsky?'

The woman with him smiled alluringly, her eyes shining, her body moving almost imperceptibly, as if hinting, promising.

The count noticed that she looked from one man to the other. As though, he thought, she is weighing us up. He had a yearning to know the thoughts that were going through her mind. Lascivious ones, he decided, and smiled back at her.

'I would be pleased,' Peter responded. 'I've nothing to rush back for.'

The cruel streak in him took pleasure in thinking of Mariella still tied out on his balcony, her backside cool to the touch.

How nice it will be to place my hot groin against it and have her again before I sleep tonight.

But for now he was smiling at the man who might have the icon. By the looks of them, he judged they might be giving him more than just coffee or brandy tonight.

A crewman played night watchman as they made their way aboard the sailing yacht, *Cartouche*.

Peter was not a sailing man and did not particularly care

for the way the ground moved beneath his feet as the vessel rose and fell on the swell.

'I think there's a storm coming,' Hans remarked as he passed his cloak to his valet.

Peter showed some surprise at the size and luxuriousness of the vessel's saloon. The walls were warm with the glow of Burmese teak. The floor was carpeted in a rich wool in a blend of navy with a thin red line running through it.

'Are you a man of some discernment?' Hans asked him suddenly. 'And of some adventure?'

Peter caught the look that passed between the Dutchman and the woman Tanya. Wide mouth smiling, she lowered her eyes as though she were sweetly innocent, which of course she definitely was not.

Peter nodded. 'I have taste and discernment in a great many things, sir. Especially in women and matters of the flesh. And also in art, collecting, antiques. Those sort of things.'

At a signal from the Dutchman, the valet took a deep rosewood box from a side shelf, opened it, and offered it to his master. Hans took a cigar. Peter did the same. They both lit up. The valet disappeared, and Tanya seemed to melt into the shadows. She was still with them, but took no part in their conversation except as a subject.

'Are you in any rush to get back, my dear count?'

Peter thought of Mariella, then of the icon. He shook his head. 'No. As I said earlier, I have nothing to get back for.'

Suddenly, it was absolutely true. It no longer mattered if some peasant did take advantage of Mariella's vulnerable position. This was one of the men who might have the icon. Besides, it looked as if something more exciting than supper might be on the menu.

'Let me show you what I have,' leered Hans. 'Tanya will follow on behind.'

Hans led him along a companionway, or a corridor, as landlubbers would term it. As in the saloon, the walls were lined with warm coloured wood. Brass-rimmed lights were set into small recesses.

Luxurious as the yacht was, the shoulders of the broad Dutchman brushed against the walls as they passed.

'In here,' he said at last. There was a look of pride on his face.

Peter, leisurely with his movements, but excited that he might at last find what he was seeking, followed his host into the room.

'These are my treasures,' Hans explained.

Peter's eyes lit up as he scrutinised the contents of the room.

'I like gold,' Hans explained. 'No matter what it has been fashioned into, I like gold. But of course, this is only a small part of my collection. Most is at my villa on the island of St Perra. If I kept it all on *Cartouche*, she would sink.'

Peter tried to control himself, but it was hard not to stare. The room dazzled. There were statues of Greek gods, goddesses, heroes and philosophers. The tails of two dolphins were entwined around each other, their noses pointing towards the ceiling, their tails towards the floor.

There were naked lovers, some in classical poses, and some more vigorously, more lewdly occupied.

There were three icons along the wall. Peter's heart leapt in his chest.

'Do you like icons?' Hans asked.

Peter's eyes narrowed as he carefully considered what to say.

'Yes,' he slowly said. 'I like icons best of all.' Yet he could see that none of these was the one he was seeking. 'Are these all you have?' he asked.

Hans nodded. 'Yes. Icons are not really my favourite item. In fact, I am seriously considering selling these and some other items.' He narrowed his eyes and puffed on his half-finished cigar. 'But the icons. Are you interested?'

Hiding his disappointment, Peter glanced over his shoulder and smiled at Tanya who was standing near the door.

'I might be,' he answered. But he really was not.

The Dutchman's eyes slid between the dark Russian and the voluptuous Tanya.

'And what about Tanya. Are you interested in her?'

A broader smile than before now creased the face of the amiable Dutchman. He took his cigar from his mouth and used it to indicate the woman who had followed them in.

Peter turned round. His eyes darkened, then a slow, sinister smile spread across his face in that lop-sided way of his.

Whilst they had talked about gold and icons, Tanya had disrobed. She was completely naked, her big breasts heaving with anticipation. He could hear her breathing, could quantify her lust.

His eyes lit up when he saw that her sex had been defoliated. Somehow a woman with no pubic hair looked far more vulnerable, far more submissive than one with.

'We can do anything we like to her,' the Dutchman said. 'Anything at all. She likes being tied up. Likes having two men rather than one.' He paused. 'Are you game?'

For a moment, Peter gave no reaction at all. Before he spoke, he smiled. 'Game? Oh yes. Game is a word I like very much.'

'That is good.'

The big Dutchman narrowed his eyes, then tapped his finger against one particular icon. 'This one here might interest you more than you think, but first, I will let you in on one of my little secrets. I truly believe, you see, that you are a man of discernment.'

Peter disliked people talking in such an abstract way, but he continued to smile politely and show interest in whatever Hans van der Loste wanted to show him.

'I like the movies, you know,' Hans proclaimed as he took hold of Peter's arm in a friendly way and led him to a door that was almost invisible among the wooden panelling of their elegant surroundings.

'This room has been decorated in the style of my favourite film!' Hans opened the door with a great flourish and a wide smile.

If he'd had a group of trumpeters, Peter mused, he would have used them to blast out a fanfare.

Smug and still smoking, Hans gestured that Peter should go first.

Peter entered, Hans near at his elbow. The naked Tanya followed on behind, her perfume suddenly more pungent, more arousing once Peter had seen the room before him.

'On a boat?' Peter exclaimed, face full of amazement and questioning.

'Why not?' Hans responded.

'Well! Well! Well!' Peter smiled and his eyes glittered as he looked around the room. 'I know someone who would like this,' he added.

Chapter 17

The Café Noir Nuit had a small frontage consisting of one door and one shop-style window whose dark green frame was divided into separate arches. Tables and chairs of a spindly metal design, the sort rising artists called cubism or abstract, sat empty and waiting out on the pavement. By day they might be well filled, but this evening all life and attraction were confined to the interior of the Café Noir Nuit.

Amber lighting spilled from the window and out onto the pavement, intensifying each time a customer opened the door to arrive or leave the premises. The sound of an accordion playing something a little dated and extremely French also drifted into the small square in which the café was situated.

The fact that the music was not up to the minute ragtime or Charleston caused Mariella to hesitate. Was this a café of the old type where only men and women of a 'professional' nature were welcome?

It was hard to tell.

Best go in, she told herself.

Smoothing her dress down over her lean hips, she took a deep breath, then pressed her hat more firmly down on her shingled bob and quickly assessed the way she looked.

Whilst collecting her clutch bag from her room, Mariella had found time to slip on a clean pair of cami-knickers and a fresh dress of pale pink. The dress had soft pleats that fell from her hips, and she wore a pretty pink hat to match and a string of pale grey pearls.

'In the pink!' she exclaimed with a small whoop of triumph as she caught sight of herself in a window. Good enough. She did not look like a prostitute.

Mariella pushed open the door to the Black Night Café half expecting all heads to turn and look over the stranger who had entered. The place buzzed with noise. People laughed, talked, sang and shouted.

Rotund waiters carrying trays of drinks, their brows sweating with effort, made their way quickly from table to table, setting down their loads, taking money, but having no respite before some other table attracted their attention.

No one gave her over-generous attention. She was just another face in the crowd, another body squeezing through the ones already there.

Although this part of the café glowed with light and life, she could see a shaded area towards the rear of the premises. Seen through an archway, shadowy shapes danced to the sound of the accordion.

The archway itself had been painted on the café side to resemble the crumbling ruins of the Coliseum in Rome; brickwork showed through crumbling plaster, and ivy entwined around sculpted heads that were painted against a sky of ultramarine.

She bumped into a waiter who she had not seen.

'Oh, I'm so sorry,' she exclaimed. She looked up into a pair of warm brown eyes. For a brief moment, her mouth hung open. Did she know this man? She decided not. He was familiar, in the same way that a dream is familiar or a half-imagined memory.

His smile was as warm as his eyes, full of friendship, the sort only found between friends of long standing.

'My fault, mademoiselle. I should have been looking where I was going. Do you require a table?'

'Yes,' she nodded. 'Yes, I do.'

Her voice was half lost in a sudden burst of laughter from a group behind her, but the waiter had obviously heard her. She continued to stare at him.

'Follow me, mademoiselle,' he said, and beckoned that she follow.

He led her to where a single table and two chairs were squeezed into a small alcove between the dance floor and the main body of the café.

Carefully tightening her stomach, Mariella squeezed into the chair that was behind the table and nearest the wall. She sighed with relief once she was sitting down, but once settled, her attention went back to the waiter. It was hard not to stare.

She was just about to thank him, when the tray he had been carrying and which she had so nearly knocked out of his hand, was placed on the table between them. To her greater surprise, he sat down in the chair opposite, his smile and the warm gleam in his eyes still intact.

'For you,' he said, pointing to the bottle of red wine and the two glasses on the tray.

'But I didn't order a bottle of wine!' she exclaimed with a laugh.

'On the house,' he returned. 'From me to you.'

Mariella sat with her mouth open, unsure what to say next, unsure of the odd confusion she was feeling inside. Where had she seen this man?

She said nothing but took the glass he offered her. As she took her first sip, she studied him over the rim of her glass. Like Peter he had dark hair and dark eyes, though with a softer expression than her lover's. He also had a slightly sardonic look that was more fleeting than Peter's and touched with humour rather than cruelty.

'Why are you staring at me?' he asked. His smile remained.

Mariella flustered. 'I . . . I . . . just thought I'd seen you somewhere before.'

She drowned her confusion in another sip of wine.

'I seem familiar to you?'

She nodded, looked at him, then to her own surprise blushed and looked away.

In an effort to hide her confusion, her gaze went to the dark red liquid in her glass. She was aware of an excited tingle starting somewhere beneath her heart, shooting like a dart to her loins, then spreading all over her body.

But why should she feel like that just because he looked a little like Peter?

She frowned thoughtfully and ran her finger around the rim of her glass.

'Good wine,' she said, then lifted her glass and swallowed another mouthful.

'Le Premier Cru,' he said slowly, seductively, his eyes never leaving her face. 'Like a beautiful woman, it is picked at full bloom, its sweetness savoured. Such is its potency, that one glass, one bottle even, is not enough.'

She was aware of his fingers upon her hand, his touch gentle, subtle, arousing. She swallowed hard; as if she could digest the sensations his looks and his touch aroused in her.

'So what do you recommend, garçon?'

He leaned so close to her, that she had a strong urge to trace the curves of his upper lip, the indent in his chin, the dark silkiness of his lashes. He took her hand between both of his.

'I recommend more of all the things you enjoy in life. But, beware of that which seems to be Premier Cru, yet is only of a secondary harvest. Such a vintage deceives the tongue and depends on the mind for its stature. Quaff only of the best, mademoiselle. You will not be disappointed.'

Spellbound, Mariella stared at him wide eyed, aware that his words were describing more than just wine. Her heart was beating madly. Her mouth was dry.

At last, her gaze linked with his, she found her voice. She smiled.

'Then pour, garçon. Pour.'

'Etienne,' he said in a voice that was not loud but carried easily over the throbbing noise of the café. 'Call me Etienne, and I will call you . . . ?'

'Mariella,' she replied, as more of the red burgundy slid into her glass. 'Call me Mariella.'

His lips moved as he mouthed her name. She imagined him saying it in the darkness, his head beside her on the pillow.

Without his gaze leaving her face, he raised his glass to meet hers, sipped the dark wine, then licked his lips and said her name again.

'Mariella.' He said it during a lull in the noise, so this time she heard him although his voice no more than a hushed breath.

Mariella's laughter was the pealing of fairy bells. This lovely young man was making her feel more vibrant, more youthful than she had felt for a long time. Suddenly, Peter and the task he had set her seemed to melt away in the warmth of the café where the smell of rich wines mixed with that of newly baked bread, strong cheeses, equally strong herbs, and the continuous fug from chain-smoked cigarettes.

Mariella glanced at the other waiters and a strong-faced woman with jangly earrings behind the bar. Occasionally the woman stared in their direction. Mariella made a quick guess at the reason why.

'Etienne,' she muttered, a worried look coming to her eyes. 'Please don't lose your job on my account.' There was genuine concern in her voice.

He smiled as he shook his head, and a lock of dark hair fell over his brow.

His mouth came closer to her, so close that she could smell the wine on his breath and the mix of masculine smells that aroused her sexuality.

His fingers were soft and gentle on her cheek.

'Please be assured. I will not lose my job.' His voice was like black velvet.

Something shiny caused Mariella's eyes to leave his face and travel to the hand he was now retrieving. She caught hold of his fingers and laid them across her palm and stared down at his hand.

'That is a very pretty object for a mere waiter to be wearing,' she exclaimed, and tapped the gold ring he wore on the third finger of his right hand. It had a ruby in one corner, an emerald in the other.

A strange silence seemed to come upon him as his gaze too went to where she was looking.

'It was my father's,' he explained in a more subdued voice than before. His eyes flickered now. She detected a note of sadness in his voice. 'He gave it to my mother before he sent her away.'

Mariella raised her eyebrows and her smile lessened. A look of melancholy came to Etienne's eyes. His voice was tinged with regret, but also hinted at anger.

Mariella sat silently, wanting to speak, yet cautious as to how she should continue. Curiosity vied with sympathy. Would it be wise to ask him the reason for his sudden change of mood? No, she told herself, and neither would it be polite. He needed distracting.

'Will you dance with me?' she said suddenly.

Without waiting for his answer, she got up from the table, her hand reaching for his.

He held her close, one hand holding hers, one arm around her waist. The tingling his presence had aroused in her did not go away and the silence between them persisted. Mariella rested her head on his shoulder, longing to take things further, but unwilling to do so until he had regained his earlier mood. In the meantime, she enjoyed the closeness of his body, the feel of his hand in her hand, his other hand on her back.

Gliding around the dance floor was a unique experience. It was almost as though they had left the more brightly lit world of reality behind. The dance area was darker, its lighting subdued.

Other bodies glided by; sleepy, satisfied voices hummed the romantic tune the accordionist was now playing. But the other dancers seemed no more than the shadows they threw on the plain walls around them, shadows created by the amber glow from where people talked, ate and drank their fill.

Their cheeks touched as they danced, and they danced as if they were one.

Mariella closed her eyes and let the music and his closeness ignite wonderful sensations that started when her nipples brushed against his chest. She sensed his mood had changed when he kissed her hair and hugged her more tightly. Desire increased as the hand that had held her waist slid lower to linger above one buttock.

As she danced, her buttocks moved against his fingers. A sizzling, burning heaviness erupted between her thighs. His breath became more warm against her ear.

The hand that had so politely held hers, now joined the other to rest above her other buttock, to feel her flesh, her muscles, move in time with the music.

Lovely feelings seemed to curl over her shoulders and fall, like a warm fountain, down over her back. Unable to resist the temptation, she pressed her body more firmly against his. There was a sudden hardening against her groin. It was as if there was a chunk of wood jammed between them. In an effort to stop it retreating, each pressed their pelvis firmly against the other.

'Can you slide up your dress?'

She wasn't shocked, but she was surprised. At first she only thought she had imagined the words. She looked questioningly up into his face.

He repeated the question. 'Can you slide your dress up without anyone else seeing?'

Suddenly, her flesh was burning at his suggestion. She couldn't wait to expose herself. Lips too dry to speak, she only nodded.

Carefully, so as not to attract attention, she put her hand down between them and gradually pulled up the front of her dress. As she did so, she could feel his penis pulsating against the back of her hand. Soon, her skirt was hitched up at the front, but still looked respectable at the back. The front of her stockinged thighs were now exposed to the air, though not to the eyes of those dancing.

She let her hand linger; looked into his eyes. Like hers, they were sparkling.

'Can you undo my buttons?'

His voice was like a flame against her ear. Her hand was still between them. She whispered a small yes and trembled as she did as he asked.

His eyes held hers as she slid her hand into the opening. He gasped as the tips of her fingers found his hard shaft. Beneath her pensive touch, his cock pulsated as if trying to escape her. Sighing with delight, she wound her fingers around it and closed her eyes.

She felt as thought she were floating. Her body was getting hotter. The subtle, tingling sensation between her legs was intensifying. It was as though her body were filling up with electrical energy.

'Get it out,' he said softly as his breath became nothing more than rushed, excited gasps. 'Get it out and slide it between your legs.'

Speechless, Mariella stared up at him. Just as she did with Peter, she was doing this man's bidding. And yet there was something different about it. There was a gentleness, a tangible affection about him, in his touch, his voice and the way he looked at her.

Carefully, so as not to injure him and not to arouse the suspicion of the other dancers, she slid his penis out through the gap in his trousers. She could easily have fainted with pleasure as the tip of his weapon nudged beneath the flimsy crotch of her pink silk knickers.

The lips of her slit divided as the moist head prodded into her furrow. A curling, rushing, shifting feeling seemed to flow from her vagina as his penis ran the length of her slit.

'Stay close,' he demanded, his arms tight around her.

She did just that. Her head lay on his shoulder. Both hands

were now clasped at the nape of his neck. His hands now completely covered her buttocks, his fingers digging into her flesh as he held her tightly against his own body.

All the time, as she danced, her thighs rubbed against his penis. In return, his penis tantalised her sex, continually hot and hard against her.

Soon she was moaning against his ear. To anyone listening, they might have thought she was humming the accordion tune like some of the other dancers. Only Etienne knew beside herself that she was approaching an orgasm with every step she took.

The first tinglings of climax stirred in her pink petalled flesh. His penis throbbed and rubbed against her in a constant rhythm in time with their dancing.

Small sounds of pleasure escaped her lips and with each step towards orgasm, she tensed then trembled against him.

Through narrowed eyes, she sometimes glanced at the other dancers. They were all too wrapped up in themselves to notice anyone else. What would they think, she wondered, if they knew that as she danced something hot and hard was making her legs tremble far more than any tune could do.

Her attention to the dancers was short lived. She looked up into Etienne's face. His jaw was tense and there was a faraway look in his eyes. He was looking at her, yet his breathing and the look in his eyes told her he was very affected by what he was doing with his cock.

For a moment it appeared that the romantic music would stop and they would be left clasping each other, their bodies still jerking regardless of the fact that there was no longer any music.

But the accordionist liked the sound of his own music. Without giving his audience a chance to stop and applaud, he immediately began playing a faster tune whose beat vaguely resembled a tango.

The tune had a constant beat, a heady mix of old and new.

Unwilling to let her partner go, Mariella clasped him closer and he did the same to her.

The tempo had increased, and with it, so had their libido.

They moved in time to the beat of the music and the dictates of their bodies.

They seemed to become one, their hips jerking against each other as they glided around the floor.

The hot prick that nestled between Mariella's legs began to do its work.

Soon she was shuddering, her eyes closed, her voice a long, soft wail of delight as the warmth of her juices covered his shaft.

'I'm coming,' she whispered against his ear.

He only groaned in reply and she soon knew why.

Etienne himself tensed against her, relaxed, tensed, relaxed and tensed again.

With each thrust of his hips, his semen spurted out of him, clung like spilt milk to her pubic hairs, the residue dripping like pearl drops into the crotch of her knickers, a few drops even dripping to the floor.

'I too have come,' he whispered back.

He brought his hands up to her face, held her and kissed her lips.

'I hope it was as good for you as it was for me,' he said softly.

Again, Mariella was speechless. Her breasts were still heaving with exertion. So many emotions had been aroused. So many new confusions had arisen.

They walked along the shoreline afterwards, a strip of sand and shingle between the quay and the headland. Both were silent, occupied with their own thoughts.

It was as though, thought Mariella, I have reached a new start in my life. But she couldn't quite work out why. And what about Peter, she asked herself? How would he view my liaison with a common waiter?

As they strolled, Etienne's arm was around her, hugging her

closely. She looked up into his face, saw it in profile against the evening clouds. He had a strong face, a man's chin. His eyes were clear and looked straight ahead. His cheekbones were high, his mouth well defined.

I want to see him again, she thought to herself. I *have* to see him again.

Etienne suddenly stopped and turned towards her.

'I want to meet you again. Will you come to the Café Noir Nuit tomorrow night?'

A spark of happiness lit up her eyes. 'Oh yes.' Then she remembered Marseilles and her promise to Joe Carey and also to Peter. Sad faced, she turned away from him. 'I can't,' she replied. 'I've promised to do something in Marseilles.'

His fingers touched her cheek. Automatically, without him having to apply any undue pressure, he turned her head to face him.

'Are you sure you cannot meet me?'

The temptation was very powerful. How easy it would be to say, yes, I will see you. It was what she wanted. She wanted it very much indeed. But she owed Peter a few favours. Going to Marseilles with Joe Carey was one that was easily repaid.

'Not tomorrow,' she repeated.

'Saturday?' He tried to look casual about his question, but Mariella could see the anxiety in his face.

He really wanted to see her. And she wanted to see him just as much. She nodded.

'All right. Saturday night should be fine. Shall we shake on it?' she asked with a smile.

He shook his head slowly, just as slowly as the smile that spread across his face.

'Shake? No. I think I can manage something far better than that.'

He took her hand and drew her down a set of damp steps that led from an expanse of shingle to an expanse of sand.

She watched as he put his coat down for her. There was a moment of pregnant silence as they looked at one other, each knowing what they would be doing next and wanting to savour the moment, take it slowly like sucking ice through a straw.

Mariella threw her bag and hat onto the sand. Her dress and underclothes followed suit.

'You didn't have to . . .' murmured Etienne, his gaze dancing over her body, lingering on the swell of her breasts, the soft pinkness of her nipples, and the golden fleece that clung in a small patch just beneath her belly.

'Oh yes I did,' she whispered, and suddenly felt almost virginal. She thought of Joe. Maybe he had seen something in her that no one else had. Perhaps this was what Etienne was seeing too.

He reached out and followed the curve of one breast with his fingers. She could see him swallowing fiercely as his fingers took hold of each nipple. He squeezed them so that they stood out that much further.

'Lovely,' he murmured.

His fingers went down to her fleece.

Mariella murmured a long, low moan as his fingers played with her golden thatch, gasping as one finger slid between her pubic lips.

She gasped even more when he fell to his knees before her.

Throwing back her head in rapture, she gave a long, low moan as his lips kissed her golden fleece, and the tip of his tongue licked her bud of passion.

She rested her fingers on his head, lost in the beautiful sensations caused by his lips and his tongue.

It was as though he were lapping her, then drinking her, devouring her pussy and the juices it was so copiously producing.

Her moans persisted, and much as she was enjoying what he was doing, the thought of what had been between her legs in the café would not go away.

'I want you!' she exclaimed at last. 'I want you to put your cock in me.'

His mouth left her. He looked up at her and was about to get to his feet. But Mariella came down to him.

Naked, she laid herself out on his coat, her eyes fixed on his flies as he fetched out the delectable rod that had done her so much good earlier.

He loosened his tie, opened his shirt, then lay down with her. He explored her body with his hands and his eyes.

She arched her back as his fingers prised apart her pubic lips. He lowered his head one last time to lick at her clitoris and the soft folds of flesh that surrounded it. Then he mounted her, and she felt the heat of him between her thighs, the hardness of him as he entered her body.

As the pleasure of his body on hers became almost too good to bear, she looked up at the stars and wished this night could last forever.

Like the waves and the shore, they came together, surging and ebbing until the last sensations had died away.

It was only as she lay there smiling and looking at the stars that something unique struck her.

The first time ever, she thought to herself. The very first time.

Valentino had not intruded on her thoughts. She had not summoned her favourite fantasy in order to achieve her orgasm. With Etienne there had been no need for her sheik to come striding into her mind.

Something different had happened between them.

Chapter 18

Geometric shapes in dark brown on beige formed the main pattern of the marble floor in the hotel foyer.

Mariella, Etienne still in her head, skipped from one to another in time with the last accordion tune she had heard at the Café Nuit Noir.

Both the tune and her light-heartedness began to fade as the lift ascended. By the time she was approaching her room, her steps were more subdued and the tune in her head seemed too distant to remember.

Would Peter have noticed she was missing?

In all likelihood, yes, and he wasn't likely to be pleased about it.

Fingers seeming to have turned to butter, she fiddled with the door key, dropping it, picking it up, and trying again. Eventually, she succeeded. She held her breath as she pushed it open.

The room was in darkness. All the same, she knew he was there. The smell of French cigarettes hung in the air. She narrowed her eyes and tried to focus. She saw the red glow of a burning cigarette, and in its instant, short-lasting light, she saw him.

Mariella's heart beat faster. A fine patina of sweat covered her skin. He was here, this man who she had never been able to resist, and now she didn't want him to be here.

But she swallowed her fear. Pretend Etienne never happened, she told herself. Don't give him away. Don't give in.

'Peter?' she said softly.

'Who interfered with my game?'

'I don't know. Truly I don't. He was gone before I caught sight of him.'

Smoke rose in spirals around his head. Silence hovered like a halo over each of them.

Mariella stood rooted to the spot, hands clenched at her sides, mouth tightly shut, eyes staring at the burning cigarette, the smoke and the presence of her lover.

'Where did you go after this person released you?'

His voice was cold.

Smoke curled, made shapes like question marks before disappearing through the open door of the balcony. His features were in silhouette because the light was behind him.

Mariella became hesitant in her movements, yet she yearned to show she was no longer in awe of him. Setting her bag down on a table, she turned away, gazing into a mirror as she took off her hat.

'I was hungry. I went to a café.'

'Alone?'

'Yes. Alone.'

'I do not believe you. I can tell from the tone of your voice that you were not alone.'

'I went alone. I swear it.'

Mariella rubbed the back of her neck as she regarded her reflection. Peter's voice and his cool detachment still held a fascination for her. He was like a snake, a wily, hypnotic snake that was as fascinating as it was dangerous. She felt that old tremor of arousal course down her spine, just as it had earlier with Etienne. And yet, with Etienne the tremor was like feathers running over her flesh. With Peter it was sharper, almost painful.

Within the mirror, she saw him rise from his chair and come to stand behind her.

She studied his reflection, the blackness in his eyes that seemed to slice into her very soul. Despite her earlier feelings of rebellion, she now felt totally helpless; back in his power.

She lowered her eyes as his hands came to rest on her shoulders. His nails dug through the thin stuff of her dress.

'Tell me where you have been. There's a good little babushka.'

All resistance flowed out of her. It was as though someone had sucked her bones from her body.

'I told you the truth. I went to get something to eat.'

'With the room attendant who released you?'

She looked quickly up at him.

'How do you know it was a room attendant?'

He shrugged. 'Who else?'

'I didn't see his face – not the room attendant I mean.'

Peter smiled a wicked, searching smile. Creases appeared at the sides of his eyes as his smile widened.

'Did he make love to you, Mariella? Did he fuck you?'

Mariella tensed, but managed to shake her head. 'No. He did not. He released me, then he was gone.'

She winced as his nails dug more sharply into her shoulders. She absorbed the pain, willing herself not to cry out as he wanted her to. At one time she would have absorbed it and turned it to pleasure by using her mind and her fantasies. But things had suddenly changed, she had changed, and she wasn't quite sure why, except that Etienne had something to do with it.

'What café did you go to? Where was it?'

She winced again, drawing in her breath, but willing herself not to cry out. This was Peter, determined to prise the truth out of her. But tonight things were different.

'It was along the quay. The big one with the trimmed pear trees outside, in the red pots.'

He tensed and for a moment, she thought he hadn't believed her. Then he relaxed slightly.

'And you dined with no one?'

She shook her head, her eyes meeting his in the mirror.

For the first time ever, she lied to him. 'No one.' She thought of Etienne, thought of what they had done on the dance floor and what they had done on the beach afterwards. The memory made her tingle with delight. This was one sexual encounter she would not allow him to take pleasure from. 'No one,' she repeated.

Still with the cigarette burning between his fingers, Peter covered her breasts with his hands and squeezed them. His lips brushed her neck and she murmured with pleasure. This was the side of Peter she found difficult to resist. She hoped against hope that he wouldn't ask her the same question again.

Thankfully, he did not pursue the matter. He merely rubbed her breasts in the way she loved, then slid one hand down over her pretty pink dress until his fingers were kneading, and pressing, and pinching at her sexual lips.

Like an instrument, he strummed her, played her, had her moaning in a low voice, had her crying out in a high one.

With his fingers alone he was controlling her, using her, making her come. Just as her orgasm was about to spill from her flesh, he asked her the same question again.

'Did you meet someone, Mariella? Did you?'

'No!' she cried out as she climaxed against his hand, her hips writhing wildly. 'No! Only waiters! Nothing but waiters.'

To Mariella's surprise, Peter did not stay with her that night but went to his own room.

'You have to keep yourself fresh, my darling,' he explained as he held her face in his hands and lightly kissed her lips. 'Tomorrow you go to Marseilles with the young American. Find out exactly where the icon is. I will do the rest.'

She knew now that he meant to steal it. At first she had been under the impression he was going to offer the American money for it. Now she knew the truth.

Peter was a difficult habit to give up, but things were happening that made her question her life with him. The count was obviously a man who appealed to the darker side of her nature, the side that needed reality to be close to fantasy. But she was changing, he realised that. It was just a question of cutting the threads that bound her to him. It wouldn't be easy, but she knew it had to be done.

She sighed with relief once the door had closed behind him,

then flopped down into a chair, her arms hanging loosely over its sides.

I did it, she thought to herself, closing her eyes as she rested her head against the back of the chair. I really did it. A nagging worry came to her. She only hoped that the icon was indeed in Marseilles. If it wasn't, it meant she would have to beguile her way onto the Dutchman's boat as well. At one time, the thought of discovering a man's weakness would have excited her. Tonight she was less enthusiastic.

There was only one thing to do in order to arouse her flagging desires.

Closing her eyes, she began to pull her dress up to her waist. Raising her hips, she wriggled out of her knickers and tossed them to one side. Except for her shoes and stockings, she was naked from the waist down.

Opening her legs, she felt the lips of her sex separate so that her inner flesh was exposed to the night air. She ran her fingers over the silky flesh, feeling its slickness, the aching hardness of her clitoris, the seeping moistness of her vagina.

The smell of Peter's cigarette still hung in the air. But behind her closed eyelids it was not Peter who was smoking, but Valentino, her sheik.

'You will stay like that for as long as I desire,' he stated, his voice forceful, his eyes full of fire.

'Let me go,' she called out, but her tone was half-hearted, her effort futile.

Three saddles had been placed side by side. She was stretched back over all three of them, naked from the waist down, her sex exposed, but a veil thrown across her face. Her wrists were tied to the saddle horns, her ankles to the wooden stands on which the saddles sat.

'I will come to use you whenever I desire,' he growled, his hand pressing against her sex, his fingertips teasing the entrance to her vagina. 'And you will accommodate me. You cannot refuse.'

She shivered at the sound of his words, the demand in his

voice. Of course she would accommodate him. Of course she wouldn't refuse.

Peter's room was in darkness. He was standing at the open door of the balcony, gazing out at the harbour lights and the luxury yachts bobbing about in the bay. On the headland, a warning light blinked on and off.

The glow of yet another cigarette burned red as he drew on it. It dimmed as he took it away. Smoke that he blew out of the door was blown back into his face by an onshore breeze. His eyes were narrowed.

So, he thought to himself, the time has come. He had known automatically that she had been lying to him. Sad that their liaison was coming to an end, but nothing lasts for ever, he thought to himself.

Women were easily acquired and easily disposed of. Mariella was no different from any other he had seduced when still a nubile virgin. That was how he liked them. Virgins. Waiting to be plucked. Once plucked they became drunk with the dark desires that he aroused in them.

For now he still needed her. Tomorrow she was going to Marseilles with the young American. Once she had reported back he would know whether the icon was in his possession or not. If it was, he would make plans to get it back. If it wasn't then he would direct his attention to Hans van der Loste, the decadent Dutchman whose woman Tanya was such a willing participant in every kind of adventurous sex.

A seed of curiosity had been planted in the mind of the Dutchman. Peter had told him of Mariella, of what she liked him to do to her, what they could both do to her together, and what they could have Tanya do to her.

The pale skin of the Dutchman had turned an excited pink. He had almost been dribbling at the mouth, and the eyes of his permanent concubine, Tanya, had gleamed with the light of wicked apprehension.

'I will sell her to you,' he had said, 'once I have finished with her.'

The big Dutchman had laughed loudly and slapped his shoulders vigorously enough to crush them.

'It is a deal,' he said. 'Name your price.'

Peter knew exactly what price he would ask.

'I have heard tell you collected a large number of Russian treasures in the years following the revolution. Obviously, Russia being the country of my birth, I am very interested in such things. I am quite willing to exchange one valuable item for another.'

A smile fixed on his face like some garish mask, the Dutchman stared him out. 'Name what you want,' he said, his teeth still smiling even when he was speaking. 'Deliver the girl to me, and I will let you choose whatever you want from my collection.'

Well satisfied with the deal, Peter nodded, his slanting eyes never leaving the blond man's face. 'My particular interest is icons,' he said. 'I am quite willing to cover any shortfall in value you may perceive between an icon and the girl. Does that sound fair to you?'

For a moment the Dutchman looked unwilling to consider such a thing. His look caused Peter to finger the slim knife he always carried in his right-hand pocket. Then the man's face relaxed. He pouted as he nodded, then he laughed.

'Yes. Yes. I see the joke now. A gold icon for a living one. How very fascinating. How very convenient.'

Flicking his spent cigarette out of the window, Count Peter Stavorsky smiled into the darkness.

Chapter 19

Pleasure boats bobbed at anchor in Old Harbour, Marseilles. As in St Asaph, many restaurants and cafés clustered around the semi-circle that formed this part of the city.

Unlike St Asaph, this part of Marseille had a more cosmopolitan atmosphere. The air was filled with the pungent aroma of Turkish coffee, lavender, and a rich compote of Oriental spices. Conversations in a mix of tongues ebbed and flowed around the tables of the pavement cafés and in the fashionable squares which although not as splendid as Vienna, had a vibrant charm all of their own.

Sometime in its history, Marseilles had been earmarked for settlement by the same Arabs who had colonised Granada in Southern Spain. They had been defeated, and yet Marseilles had a more alien, more exotic atmosphere than any other French city.

Joe had been delighted to see Mariella again. He was like a child that has only just discovered the intricacies of a clockwork train.

Even in the car on the way down, his eyes had been filled with a kind of awe, wanting to touch her, yet still seeming surprised that she would allow him to.

'Do you mind?' he had asked her breathlessly, his hand hovering just inches from her breast.

She had looked at him, thought of Peter, thought of Etienne; then thought of herself. She smiled and let her arms fall listlessly to her side.

'Be my guest.'

His eyes had been full of wonder. He had gasped at the feel of her, the firmness of her flesh beneath the softness of the cream and blue light wool outfit she was wearing. The top she wore came complete with the modern wide-legged trousers – the most daring thing to happen in years. From a place called Hollywood, the assistant had told her in the Paris fashion house where she had bought it.

As his hand wandered beneath the hip-length tunic that teamed with the pants, Mariella toyed with the notion that the reason Jean Harlow wore tunic tops and trousers was in order that her lovers could more easily get at her breasts.

Who cares, she thought. I like them. Then, both comforted and aroused, she sighed and closed her eyes. Only the thin silk of her camisole remained between her breast and the warmth of his hand.

Mariella looked up into his eyes, sighing with pleasure as his fingers did lovely things to her nipples.

'That is so delicious,' she sighed. 'I never thought anything could be so wonderfully pleasant.'

Joe swallowed, his eyes wide with wonder. 'Oh, my darling!' he exclaimed before falling on her, his lips showering her with kisses. Breathless, he at last let her go. He held her at arm's length and looked at her thoughtfully.

'We are almost at the museum. I don't want to rush this.'

Taking his point, Mariella smoothed her tunic back over her breasts and her hips. She kissed his cheek then stroked it.

'But you won't deny me the pleasure – after we have had a good look around the museum, of course.'

Breathless still, he shook his head. 'No. I won't.'

A sudden blast of air sounded from the hearing tube between the passenger compartment and the chauffeur. Joe unplugged it and snapped a nervous 'yes'.

'We are here, monsieur,' muttered a muffled voice.

'Thank you, Pierre.'

'It is not Pierre, monsieur. He has a malade. It is Henri.'

'Then thank you, Henri,' Joe added. With one impatient stab, he replaced the plug into the hearing device. 'We are here,' he repeated, turning his attention directly to Mariella who was staring at the hearing device and looking puzzled. 'What are you frowning for? Is something wrong?'

He sounded genuinely concerned.

Mariella stopped frowning and smiled instead. 'Nothing is wrong,' she said brightly. 'Nothing at all.'

Her heart was thumping as the chauffeur opened the car door. Joe got out first and offered her his hand. She took it, her face flushing with the effort of smiling at him rather than looking into the face of the chauffeur. Yet she had to see the face of this man whose voice had seemed so familiar.

One hand rested on the door. Her eyes settled on it presuming she'd recognise him from that alone. Her heart dropped. His hand was gloved.

The moment came for her to thank him for opening the door. It was only polite. She waited, counted the seconds for the right moment, her heart pulsing with excitement.

Her smile was sweet. Her eyes sparkled. She looked up into his face expecting to see . . . ?

He stared straight ahead. He had very bushy eyebrows, a large nose and a thick moustache. His cheeks had the broken-veined redness of a man who likes wine too much.

Her heartbeat slowed as her pulse returned to normal.

You fool, she remonstrated. You heard a voice and your hormones went racing. It was similar to his, yet it wasn't his. Control yourself. Concentrate on what you are doing.

'Now,' she said after taking a deep breath and looping her arm through that of Joseph Michael Carey III. 'Show me this museum of yours.'

'Sure!' he gushed. His face blushed with pleasure. 'Sure!'

He explained that the place was open to selected visitors all year round, and to the general public for four months only. At present the former arrangement was in operation.

A curator unlocked for them, his back so bent that his face was almost level with the keyhole into which he inserted the large, metal key.

The doors themselves were of light oak. Each was decorated with a sword design, its details picked out in preformed metal and pieces of blue and green stone so beloved of the Art Deco enthusiasts.

When the doors opened, Mariella found herself in a marble floored foyer. Two glass doors which depicted painted scenes of Gothic legend opened between the foyer and the main display area.

Mariella took a deep breath. The marble floor gleamed, reflecting the light from a range of arched windows set high up. The eye was urged to follow the black marble pillars that ran to fan out like the leaves of a palm tree, arching high above to support a turquoise ceiling.

'It's like a cathedral,' she said softly.

Joe grinned and hugged her more tightly. 'Mother would be thrilled to hear you say that.'

Mariella shivered.

'Are you cold?' he asked her.

Still eyeing the high ceiling, she shook her head. 'No. It's just so imposing.'

'Look here,' he said suddenly, his voice full of boyish excitement.

He took hold of her hand and pulled her through a high doorway and into a room that was darker than the main display area.

Mariella caught her breath. Egyptian hieroglyphics and stilted figures lined the walls. Black eyes stared from long-dead kings, queens, priests and deities. In the middle of the room were three sarcophagi. Ranged around the walls were articles of furniture and stone statues of the same gods who paraded around the walls.

'This stuff is incredible!' she exclaimed. 'Does it all belong to you?'

'Yep!' Joe exclaimed proudly. 'While my mother took an interest in valuable religious artefacts and stuff, I got hooked on history – especially the Egyptians. Don't they make you imagine things?'

'Oh yes.' Mariella's voice was dreamy. She trailed her

fingers over some of the more beautiful exhibits; gold cheetahs with diamond collars and eyes of green emeralds; elongated cats made of ebony, their eyes of amber.

Most imposing of all were the funeral masks; great gold things said to be in the image of their owners as they looked at death.

Mariella shuddered as she traced their eyes, their noses and their lips.

It was hard not to loiter and admire everything; to ask Joe to explain what each thing was. Instinctively, her eyes sought out only the more dramatic. There was one thing above all others that appealed to her.

Hanging like a brilliant butterfly in an alcove at one end of the room, was the most beautiful costume Mariella had ever seen.

Slowly she walked past each of the painted caskets, statues of Anubis, of Horus and the crisp wall paintings of Isis until she stood before the glowing outfit.

Joe came to stand behind her. He rested his hands on her shoulders and lightly kissed her neck.

'Do you like it?' His voice was husky, muted against her hair.

She nodded but did not answer. Her eyes were filled with the delicate beauty of the outfit. There was gold leaf on the trailing fronds that hung from the shoulders. Lapis lazuli sewn into the materials with strips of silver thread glinted like a cluster of gazing eyes.

Joe's voice echoed around the room. 'It belonged to a queen. It was found in a sealed casket beside the main tomb. Luckily no air or insects had got into it otherwise it would be no more than a bundle of powder by now.'

Mariella reached out. The cloth, so ornate with precious metals and stones, felt oddly cold, strangely fragile. 'It's beautiful,' Mariella whispered.

Joe kissed the top of her head. 'Try it on.' The flat of his hand pressed against her back. She stepped forward.

Surprised he should allow so rare an item even to be touched, she turned and looked up at him. 'Are you sure about that?'

His eyes were bright with excitement. 'Yes,' he said breathlessly. 'Please do.'

Slowly, her eyes on the glowing garment, Mariella slipped off her clothes.

Joe watched as each item was removed, his eyes wide, his breathing sounding almost painful.

Mariella was well aware that he was staring at her, so she took her time.

I'm tormenting him, she thought to herself. I'm torturing him.

With slow deliberation, she handed each item of discarded clothing into Joe's trembling hands. In turn, he laid them neatly on the nearest sarcophagus.

Shivering slightly, Mariella turned her back on him and reached for the outfit once worn by an Egyptian queen.

Her heart was thumping. Her blood was coursing through her veins like white hot heat.

In her mind, she was no longer in a museum but in the cool confines of the pharaoh's palace in Alexandria, Karnak, or Memphis.

The scene beyond the window was no longer the Rhone delta but the Nile. What sounds filtered in from the square outside might just as well have been those of three thousand years ago.

Fantasy overlapped reality as she began dressing herself in the costume of an Egyptian queen. Six Nubian slaves stood round at her disposal, yet on this occasion she had chosen to dress herself.

Silky soft, despite its great age, the skirt portion merely wrapped around her hips, fastening just below her navel. Her legs were visible from half-way down her thighs. She clipped thick anklets of gold and rubies around her ankles.

The bodice was a strap affair fashioned from gold fabric

and precious stones. It came over her shoulders, crossed over between her breasts. It supported, but did not cover them.

She looked down at her naked breasts.

'The finishing touch,' she said seductively, smiling at Joe as she pinched and pulled on each nipple.

She heard him groan; saw the lust in his eyes.

'Mariella . . .' He stepped forward.

Mariella raised her hand, palm towards him.

'Stay there. I am not finished dressing yet.'

Joe did exactly as ordered.

Mariella reached for the headdress.

The headdress was typical; the emblems of the upper and lower Nile sitting on the forehead, a stiff veil of gold fabric squared off at chin level. Around her neck she placed a thick collar of turquoise, lapis lazuli, gold, and rubies. Snakes made of solid gold with emerald eyes curled up from her wrists to her elbows.

Where the garment had rested there remained only a gold and ebony throne. Mariella mounted the two steps before it, then turned round and, like a queen, stood with head held high, chin jutting proudly. Her eyes burned into those of Joe.

'Kneel!' In her mind she had many subjects. In reality, there was only one.

The voice she adopted was one she thought a queen might well have used.

Joe stared, his mouth open, his eyes wide.

Mariella lifted her head higher. 'Did you hear me, slave? Kneel! You are my slave, here only to do my bidding. Remember that!'

An excited expression came into Joe's eyes. His cheeks turned a pale pink as his breath quickened.

Mariella pointed at him. 'Kneel!'

Slowly, Joe sank to his knees. 'Mariella!'

'Your majesty,' she said through clenched teeth. 'Call me your majesty or mistress.'

She heard him groan and saw the sudden thrust occurring

against the front of his trousers. Inwardly she smiled to herself. Now it was her in a position of power; not Peter. Not another man. This was Mariella. Queen Mariella! Outside she showed no sign of her amusement or of what she intended doing. Her expression showed no more emotion than the stiff wall paintings or the gilded death masks. Her command was sudden.

'Take off your clothes.'

Joe gasped. 'What? All of them?'

'All of them!'

Without a trace of a smile, Mariella watched as Joe removed all his clothes and placed them with hers. When his attention was diverted to the task of putting his clothes on the sarcophagus, she took the opportunity to study his erection. Like the head of a proud horse, it reared from his loins, his pubic hair a mane of tangled growth behind it. As she eyed the glistening glans that crowned his stalk, she licked her lips – but quickly so he would not see.

By the time he had turned towards her, her face was inscrutable, her arms crossed just below her chest, palms face down just above them.

Narrowing her eyes, she found it possible to enjoy the moment in actuality and in her mind.

The naked Joe knelt before her. Many naked slaves knelt in her mind. Some were black, some brown, some fair. She walked between lines of them. Every so often, she would notice the balls of one in front hung heavier than his comrades. She tapped the shoulder of each, bade them rise, then handled their equipment, pulling on their stems and weighing their balls in her hand.

She took delight in playing with some until their stems were hard, their balls retreating into their bodies as their seed spurted onto the ground.

In her mind, one spat onto the ground just in front of her foot.

His stem was big, his pubic hair very dark against the whiteness of his flesh.

'Take him to be gelded,' she snarled, her hand slapping hard against the man's face.

Only as the blood trickled from the corner of his mouth did she look him in the face and see the white scar running down his cheek.

Her thoughts crossed back from fantasy into reality. Now it was Joe kneeling before her.

Sexual sensations intensified, spreading outwards like long, thin tendrils. Although she was standing completely still, sexual arousal made her feel as though she were moving, trembling gently.

Joe's hair had fallen over his temples. There was a hint of sweat on his skin which served to make his muscles seem more defined than they would normally be. His chest rose and fell more swiftly as his breath quickened.

Mariella took the first step down from the Egyptian throne. The second brought her on a level with him.

'Mariella,' he gasped, and held out his arms.

'No! Do not touch me!' Her voice sounded suitably imperious.

As if singed by a terrible flame, his hands fell to his sides. Her eyes burned into his. His jaw moved up and down but no words came out.

'Be silent, slave!' she cried, her body seeming to burn as she warmed to her part.

The glowing, golden outfit which covered her body had also made her a queen. She could not help acting like one. It was as though the costume was dictating what she should be, what she should see and what she should do.

She felt full of fire, her mind alive with the will to command and her body with the urge to achieve pleasure.

'Stand still,' she ordered. 'Do nothing, say nothing unless I order it. Do you understand?'

Joe opened his mouth, then having caught the warning look in her eyes, closed it again. He nodded yes.

Mariella ran her hand down over his chest. As she went

further, she felt the muscles of his stomach tense beneath her touch. His penis leapt forward harder and more demanding than before. Her fingers slid under it. She squeezed his testicles with tenderness, not violence. Nevertheless, she saw him wince.

Letting go of his scrotum, she walked round him, trailing her hand over his hard thighs and the tight flesh of his buttocks. He trembled as she prised his buttocks apart. A thrill shot through her as she eyed the sight before her. It was strange to view such a taboo item, yet also thrilling. Power, she decided, was as arousing as submission.

Slowly, she walked back up to the antique throne, sat down, then draped her legs over each arm so that her sex was fully exposed.

Joe gasped, his expression one of shock that his 'virgin' was a lot more forward than he had thought.

Hands resting on her raised knees, Mariella smiled at him.

'Worship me,' she ordered, her voice as soft and husky as a brush sweeping cobbles.

Joe's eyes seemed to shoot forward out of his head. He did not, could not tear his eyes away from the pink flesh so beautifully framed by the golden hair of her pubes.

'On your knees,' Mariella ordered.

Joe's movements became stilted, as if he were an automaton made by some manic toy maker.

He dropped like a stone. Arms dangling at his side, he walked forward on his knees, his gaze fixed on the cluster of pink flesh. Her sex was acting like a magnet, drawing him forward.

When he came to the two steps he used his hands to pull himself up until his face was level with her pussy.

Her smell filled his head. It was as aromatic as fresh rose petals yet, like the sea, it hinted at danger.

'Worship me,' Mariella repeated.

Cautiously, slowly, as if he wanted to savour the moment

or be very precise about what he was going to do, Joe leaned forward, and without closing his eyes, he tasted her.

Mariella trembled as his lips sucked on her flesh and the tip of his tongue poked at her clitoris.

'That's it,' she gasped. 'That's exactly it.'

Her words gave Joe new confidence, and the taste of her only served to heighten his own desire.

He lapped at her, sucked at her, poked his tongue into her and drank of her juices, their delicacy lying at the back of his throat.

Mariella threw her head back, her moans subdued but delicious. She spread her fingers so that she could more easily play with her own breasts, her own nipples.

She felt them hardening as her pleasure increased. Sensation after sensation seemed to rise like layers of floating silk, rising higher into the sky, one after another, flashes of colour inlaid so they became another colour and still floating higher, ever higher.

In her mind, it was Peter doing this; Peter her gelded slave, his penis hard, yet bereft of the power to drive into her. He was no longer Valentino, no longer her sheik. He was now her slave and his life depended on whether his tongue was long and his sucking skilful.

Eventually, she were at her height, then suddenly she was falling, floating, sliding down to earth, just as her climax floated and slid away to almost nothing.

Once she had finished, she grabbed hold of Joe's hair and tugged his mouth away from her sex. Female body juices glistened around his mouth. His mouth hung open. He was breathing heavily.

'I have finished,' she said with a smile.

Joe looked puzzled.

Exalting in the part she was playing, Mariella shook his head, then kicked him and sent him flying across the floor.

'But I have not finished with you,' she snarled.

The kohl-edged eyes of the dead Egyptians watched as

Mariella got up from her throne and fetched a few items of makeup from her clutch bag.

Speechless, Joe remained sprawled on the floor watching and waiting for whatever she wanted to do next.

'Kneel,' she commanded.

Joe struggled back onto his knees, his hands again hanging at his sides.

Mariella could see that his phallus was aching for release. He had probably expected to mount her once she had reached her climax. He was going to be disappointed. Mariella had other plans for him.

Concentration creased her face as she applied lipstick and eye shadow to her American lover. She found an Egyptian wig that swept past his shoulders.

'You look like a woman now. Lie down,' she told him. 'I am going to have you.'

Joe, his eyes still wide with amazement and his lips quivering with meek surprise, did exactly as she commanded.

He lay down on the cold floor, his phallus stiff and upright, standing proud of his body.

Mariella took up the crook and the flail that belonged to her outfit. She used the flail to lash at his unprotected body.

Gritting his teeth, he closed his eyes tightly and accepted the blow.

He opened his eyes again when he felt the head of the crook hooked around his phallus. He moaned as she pulled it this way and that, and she smiled to think she had now got such power to make a man moan like that.

But her own libido was fast recovering, and his cock was so irresistible.

Holding herself as she had before, but now with the flail and crook in her hands, she lowered herself onto his penis. Pleasure covered her like a warm mantle as she felt the hardness of his erection enter her portal and burrow deep inside.

Then, just as if she were a man, she leaned forward and

rested her hands on the floor. She pumped at him, jerked on him, her hips ferocious with onslaught.

Joe reached for her jiggling breasts.

'No!'

Eyes staring, he let his hands fall back.

'Spread them!' ordered Mariella.

He did exactly as she asked. He spread his arms up above his head. He was not tied by rope, wire or chain, and yet he might just as well have been.

The force of her eyes and her personality held him there, controlled him as he had never been controlled before.

Mariella saw him clench his jaw. It gave her pleasure to think he was having trouble obeying her. His gaze kept dropping to her breasts. He badly wanted to touch her, yet her willpower alone was holding him at bay.

She bounced up and down on him, the lips of her sex oozing with the juice of renewed arousal. Deep in her vagina, Joe's penis began to throb. He groaned, mewed like a kitten, his voice becoming shriller as his semen rose closer to the surface.

At last it happened, a warm flush of fluid gushed from Joe's penis and filled Mariella's body.

Sweat glistened on both their bodies now as they looked at each other. Both were breathless.

'I've been a fool,' said Joe thoughtfully.

Mariella tilted her head to one side. She resembled a quizzical sparrow. 'Why is that?'

He smiled a little ruefully. 'You're not a virgin, are you?'

Now it was Mariella's turn to smile.

'Yes,' she replied. 'You could say that.'

Once they were dressed and fully satiated, they looked at the rest of the collection, a little of which had been accumulated by Joe's mother, and the rest by himself.

Mariella took particular note of the icons. There were three, all of gold, and each ornately unique from each other.

'Are these the full extent of your collection?' she asked.

He nodded a little apologetically. 'These are it, but I won't be collecting any more. They were my mother's taste, not mine. Took great joy from them, she did. Now she's gone there don't seem much point in keeping them. They'll definitely be going to auction.'

Mariella eyed each of the icons in turn just to make doubly sure that her first impression was correct. It was. Not one fitted the description given her by Count Peter Stavorsky.

Her heart sank. She was not too keen on having to strike up a relationship with the Dutchman. She was far more keen on developing the relationship she had just started with Etienne the waiter.

Chapter 20

They followed the coast road back from Marseilles and travelled for mile after mile before the yellow flatness of the Rhone delta gave way to the more curvaceous terrain of the Côte d'Azure. Green vegetation tumbled down over a sandstone rock face on one side of the road and the air smelt of lemon and wisteria. On the other side of the road, the sea was a moving tableau of green and blue interspersed by diamonds of sparkling sunlight.

Mariella lay back in her seat, eyes half closed, body relaxed. In her mind she relived what had happened back in the museum, though as the miles slipped away and they neared St Asaph, Peter came creeping back into her mind like a sticky, dark shadow.

But I have fulfilled the task, she told herself. I have found out that Joe doesn't have the icon. Peter should be pleased about that because it means that it is Hans van der Loste who has what he wants – presumably.

The sea whizzed by and for a moment she wished she was out there and not heading back to St Asaph and Peter. Hopefully, he would be pleased she had found out that Joe didn't have his precious icon. On the other hand, he might be annoyed that the quest must go on.

In an effort to push him from her mind, at least for the moment, she concentrated on the passing scenery. Diamonds of sunlight still danced over the sea, its effect hypnotically calming. Soon, Peter was pushed into the further corners of her mind. Other visions came to mind and she murmured like a woman dreaming an erotic dream and cuddled nearer to Joe, her head on his shoulder.

He turned and kissed her forehead. She closed her eyes so

she could savour the moment and perhaps provide a gateway through which an erotic fantasy could enter.

'I enjoyed what you did today,' he whispered, glancing towards their chauffeur as he did so. 'You really sounded like a queen. Sure looked like one too.'

Mariella's eyes flickered open. There was a coquettish wickedness in them as she looked into his.

'Then we'll have to do it again,' she said, her hand caressing his thigh.

Alarmed, Joe glanced meaningfully at the driver and raised his finger to his lips. At the same time he uttered a short shushing sound.

Unperturbed, Mariella pressed herself more firmly against him. 'Don't be so nervous, Joe. You weren't like this earlier when I took advantage of you; when I squeezed your balls and rode you like a man would ride a woman.'

'But . . .' he began, his face turning pink, his eyes flickering between her and the chauffeur.

Mariella pressed her finger against his lips.

'Don't be silly. He can't hear us through that glass. Isn't that why you've got that speaking device there?'

Joe looked quickly at the tube through which he had addressed the driver earlier. His smile was nervous. He shook his head.

'I am silly,' he said, still shaking his head as if he were trying to get rid of the fact. 'Of course he can't hear me.'

Mariella breathed in his scent as he hugged her close, his lips brushing her throat. His hair was like satin against her face.

She opened her eyes and looked out at the sea. Its cool greenness seemed to be reaching out to her, inviting her to come closer. Her eyes narrowed as she glimpsed long sandy beaches, their glare almost too powerful to look at.

Like a desert, she thought to herself, and remembered Valentino, her fantasy lover.

If she narrowed her eyes that much more, she could see him there, riding across the sand on his black horse, his robes flying out behind him. The sea was no longer a mass of water, but a mirage that blurred at the horizon and blended with the sky.

She had no recollection of him dismounting in her dream, yet she could see the tassels on his boots swinging ferociously from side to side as he walked towards her.

Suddenly, her heart seemed to catch in her throat. Her eyes opened a little more. Surely this dream was too vivid not to be real?

Surely she really could see a horseman galloping along the beach?

Her eyes snapped fully open. 'Please,' she said suddenly, her head raised from his shoulder. 'Can we stop and admire the view?'

Joe stopped kissing her and reached for the speaking tube. 'Why not? There's a place we can pull in just up ahead.'

The place where they stopped was edged with yellow stone and overlooked a small cove. Pieces of wood supported by roughly hewn stakes had been used to form steps down to the sandy beach.

Mariella, desperate now to find out whether she had merely been dreaming, or whether her dream lover really was galloping along the sand, kicked off her shoes and bounded away down the path like some kind of goat or gazelle.

'Hey!' shouted Joe. 'Wait for me!'

Taken off guard, Joe staggered as he pushed his shoes from his feet, closely followed by his socks. Once he had regained his balance, he too was off down the beach path.

Mariella was up to her knees in salt water by the time Joe got to her. She was shielding her eyes from the sun, her gaze raking the beach from one end to the other, as far as the eye could see.

'You're soaked,' Joe said.

Mariella merely nodded and muttered yes.

Her pant suit was indeed soaking, the thin cloth clinging to her legs and clearly defining the area in between.

Joe, too, was wet, his light flannel trousers heavy with water.

Disappointed, Mariella let her arms fall to her sides.

'He's gone,' she murmured, her eyes still gazing at the beach.

Joe glanced over each shoulder in a perfunctory manner.

'Who's gone?'

'The horseman,' she replied. 'He was dressed in black and he was riding a black horse.'

Joe stared at her and for a moment looked as if he might be questioning whether she was entirely sane. But the look didn't last. His face cracked with affability, though his laugh was a little nervous.

'Wow, but you've got a vivid imagination.'

Mariella glared. 'I was not imagining him.'

Joe shuffled from one foot to the other. 'Honey, look at the sand.' He spread his arm and gestured at the gleaming expanse of blinding white. 'Not a mark, except for our footsteps.'

Mariella followed the sweep of his arm. She frowned, blinked and shook her head, raised her hands and clenched her fists. 'He was real. I know he was real.'

Joe touched her shoulder. 'You just woke up, honey – too quickly, I think. Straight from the car, then running down those steps. Your daydream's got mixed up with real life. It happens. Why, I had a pal back in Chicago . . .'

'You're right!'

Mariella's response was quick, but also dismissive. She didn't want to hear about his old pal back in Chicago. She didn't want to dwell on the fact that her daydreams might very well be getting mixed up with reality.

'You're right,' she repeated, her whole body seeming to become as soft as the wet sand beneath her feet. 'What a fool I am. What a bloody fool!'

Shoulders slumped, she covered her face with her hands

and shook her head so that her hair tangled in her fingers.

'Oh, Mariella,' he moaned as he took her in his arms. 'I'd do anything for you. I really would.'

There was warmth in the moment, but also something else. Mariella had the faintest feeling that sometime soon she might very well need someone like Joe, someone who would do anything for her.

But for now she laughed, throwing her head back so that the sea breeze caught her hair and flung it around her head in a salt soaked tangle.

Joe picked her up and carried her to the beach. He laid her on the warm sand, her pretending to be drowned, eyes closed, arms and legs limp as though they were as waterlogged as their clothes.

Even as he stripped her clothes from her body, she did not open her eyes or move.

Soon, she was naked. The sand was warm and soothing against her back and buttocks. The sun warmed her breasts and belly.

Joe's voice was low but full of excitement as he spoke into her ear.

'Are you dead? I think you are pretending to be drowned. If so, I will have to bury you.'

She did not respond. This was her game and Joe was her playmate.

True to his role, Joe began humming the funeral march as he spread her legs as wide as he could. Then he scraped the sand away from beneath her legs and piled it over them. He did the same to her arms.

Mariella closed her eyes and smiled as the soft warmth of his hands permeated her flesh. She felt considerably relaxed. The sand had turned cool around her buried limbs. Her torso was still fully exposed. She imagined what he was seeing, a body without legs, without arms but with round, ripe breasts and a sex that was completely open to his view.

What he did next surprised her, but she did not protest. A silk handkerchief was placed over her eyes. The weight of damp sand was added, but it did not end there.

As though he were casting a mould of her cranium, he patted sand all over her head until it fitted her like a large helmet. Although she knew the sand was no real barrier to her escaping his treatment of her, Mariella let the feelings of helplessness drift over her and turn swiftly to sexual excitement.

She was trapped in soft sand, vulnerable to anything he wanted to do to her, but of course, in her mind it wasn't Joe. Her sheik had returned, and whatever Joe did, Valentino was doing too.

Her breasts rose and fell more quickly. Her nipples became as hard as small pebbles. She felt his shadow fall over her as he got down onto his hands and knees. The silky, slippery head of his penis nudged at the frills of flesh and the sensitive bud they surrounded.

Mariella held her breath. A moan of delight threatened to leave her mouth, but she held it back, caught it and left it hanging in suspension at the back of her throat. She willed herself to forget that she had a voice, limbs, even a head. At this moment in time, she was only a body, a creature constructed of those parts that give and receive sexual pleasure – the epicentres of erogenous zones.

She heard him catch his breath as he aimed his penis into her opening. Such a heat, she thought to herself as the hard, hot rod pushed smoothly into her welcoming purse. The urge to arch her back was incredibly powerful, yet she resisted. After all, she was playing dead, wasn't she?

Pubic hair and sand mingled together as the tip of his cock touched the neck of her womb. A hot tongue pushed into her mouth, licking every corner while she remained motionless, unresponsive.

Only her nipples ignored the fantasy of her mind. Encouraged by Joe's fingers, they hardened and stood out proudly from her breasts. Tingles of delight radiated out from them and made her want to shudder, to cry out for him to do more, to pull them, pinch them, and stretch them as much as he liked.

At last he tensed, his body rigid against hers as he ejaculated into her womb. Even as he did so, a great wave of release pounded throughout her own body, ebbing, flowing, then crashing in one stupendous, foam-filled climax.

Mariella's breath came in quick, sharp gasps. There was no other sign that she had orgasmed. Her body had remained completely still throughout.

'I will leave you here until I need you again,' said the sheik, and in her mind she always would be there, waiting for him to ignite her senses.

In reality, she was with Joe and both of them had climaxed.

At last she sat up, sand falling away from her head and her limbs. She laughed and shook it all away, looked down between her legs and saw her sexual honey oozing from her body and trickling on to the sand.

Sand-covered as they both were, Joe held her face and kissed her. His expression was one of admiration.

'You turn sex into adult games,' he commented. 'It's like being a child all over again. Pretending, and all that.'

'It is a game,' she responded as she shook the sand out of her soaked clothes. 'It's like playing. That's what it is. Grown up playtime.'

As she slipped into her sodden tunic top, her gaze followed the steps that led to the top of the cliff. Silhouetted against the sky, she could see a tall figure in pale grey. She frowned and pushed her hair away from her eyes. Any other chauffeur would have stayed in the car until their employer had returned, or at least, he would have avoided intruding on private goings on.

But this chauffeur was staring down at them, his body so rigid, he might just as well have been a dead tree trunk or an inanimate chunk of rock.

For a moment Mariella stared back.

'What are you looking at now?' Joe asked. 'Another black robed rider on a sturdy black horse?'

She turned to him. 'We're being watched,' she said and pointed at the top of the cliff.

Joe looked, then, smiling, shook his head and hugged her.

'Your imagination again,' he said ruefully.

Mariella looked back up. This time there was only blue sky. The chauffeur had gone.

Chapter 21

Mariella hesitated and took a deep breath before knocking at Peter's door. It was getting close to ten o'clock, one hour later than her promised time of arrival.

'Enter!'

She poked at her hair and licked her lips; another quick intake of breath before her hand dropped like a stone to the door handle.

The room was in darkness, lit only by the moon and the harbour lights. A brooding silence hung in the air broken only by the sound of her footsteps on the highly polished wooden floor.

The red glow of a burning cigarette caught her eye.

'You are late.' His tone was low and lazy.

Mariella willed herself not to shiver. She took a deep breath, thought about leaving the room and leaving him. But to think such thoughts was easier than actually doing them. The power of his presence reached out to her, held her there as easily as if she were bound by chains. He was not just part of her life, he was part of her dreams.

'Why are you late?'

'Dinner – the service was a little slow . . .'

'Take your clothes off,' he commanded.

'What? But don't you want to know—'

'No! You will tell me your exploits later. For now I wish you to take your clothes off. Do so immediately.'

Compulsively, Mariella smoothed her hands over the dress she had changed into to go out to dinner with Joe. Like her skin, it seemed to tremble with apprehension. Rebellious words that had been in her head on the way back, now melted away.

Her fingers went to the buttons that fastened the dress at the shoulders. With slow, almost mesmeric movements, she undid the buttons, removed the dress. Even once she had set it down on a chair, her fingers continued to caress the smooth, satin trim of the scalloped hemline before removing her underwear. Slowly, her fingers dropped to her garters.

'Leave your stockings on,' Peter commanded.

Mariella stood in the darkness, her gleaming body picked out by the light coming through the window. She trembled, yet held her head high, jaw jutting, but not pugnacious. Shoulders square, she held her hands at her sides, fists clenched. Her nipples tingled and grew erect. Smoke from his cigarette circled her body like threads from a silken web.

The red glow of his cigarette disappeared. The smoke rolled across the path of the light. Her eyes followed him as he rose from the chair, his shadow falling over her as he passed between her and the window.

Somehow, it was hard to turn her head, to look up into his face. But she willed herself to do it. Her will became his once she had seen the gleam of his eyes and the structure of his face half hidden by shadows. His slow, sardonic smile was the last thing she saw before he slipped the blindfold around her eyes.

'No words,' he said.

Unable to stop herself, she gasped with pleasure as his hand cupped her breast, his thumb flicking at her nipple. A burning path seemed to open in her flesh as that same hand went on down over her belly. She stood on her toes for a moment as his fingers slid between her legs.

'Open them wider,' he ordered. 'And keep still. Put your hands behind your back.'

All willpower seemed to drain away. She stared into her private darkness, knew instinctively what he was going to do even before the cord was tied around her wrists. She was powerless to stop herself from sinking back into that role he had allotted her. How had this happened, she asked herself?

Why do I let him do this? But, of course, she knew what the answer was. No one enters such an enticing web unless they wish to. She had entered, and now she was not entirely sure of the way out.

What he said and did next was unexpected.

'You will hear nothing,' he said as he fixed some kind of band over her head. 'You will see nothing. You will only feel and enjoy what I will do to you.'

Soft pads covered her ears. Her darkness was complete. Even if she had wanted to protest now, it was too late. Only her legs and mouth were free. Reality was controlled by him. Her sexuality was controlled by the fantasies of her own mind.

There was a moment of stillness, of apartness. Because she could not see or hear, it felt as though she were floating, retreating into herself. At first it was an experience to be explored, but then a great urge to communicate in whatever way possible overwhelmed her.

But Peter did not touch her. She could not see him. Neither could she hear or feel his presence.

Time became indefinite, immeasurable. After what seemed like an age, a hand covered one breast and squeezed. She gasped, wanted to cry out how grateful she was, remembering just in time that Peter did not want her to speak.

Revelling in the warmth of the palms that now covered both breasts, she thrust them outwards and groaned as they were squeezed. Her body undulated as though she were the snake and he the charmer. Not too far short of the truth, she thought to herself, but not forever; not for much longer.

Again, rather than submitting to whoever was touching her, she retreated into her fantasy. Valentino awaited her.

She remembered seeing him on the big screen, his dark eyes glaring into those of the captive woman who cowered in the corner, or merely trembled beneath his lustful gaze.

But on screen, the sheik, the part Valentino was playing, merely stole kisses, meaningful looks and passionate embraces. In the role allotted him by Mariella, he did much more than that.

In her fantasy she was dressed in the most astonishing garment that was not unlike the one she had worn in Joe Carey's museum in Marseilles.

Besides having jewelled straps that crossed between her breasts, this one came complete with gold nipple clamps encrusted with pink pearls. A single pearl drop swung from each one.

The skirt of this garment was cut much higher. More pearls were sewn into her pubic hair. One large one was sewn at the beginning of her slit so that when he entered her, it would press directly against her clitoris. As at the museum, a heavy collar rested around her neck, but this one had a chain attached, and the sheik was holding the other end of it.

'My sex slave,' he said, and she shivered with pleasure, but not just because of his words.

Reality was intruding upon her dream. One of the hands that had been caressing her breasts now ran down over her belly. She arched her back and thrust her hips forward as fingers teased the hairs that covered her pubic region.

When the hands left her body she wanted to moan, wanted to cry. She was aware of movement behind her. His hand trailed over her hip before clutching one buttock. Then both buttocks were caressed, felt and gripped. Sharp nails dug gently into her flesh. She gasped. Were Peter's fingernails really that long? The answer was immediate. His nails were short! Peter's nails were always short, well manicured and shiny with polish.

Her jaw dropped. She wanted to ask, but again remembered he'd specifically told her not to make a sound.

Was this the whole point of the game? Guessing whose hands were feeling her body, touching, giving and getting pleasure from her most secret places?

Waves of decadent desire emanated from those wandering hands. She threw her head back and moaned as the hands took hold of her buttocks, spread them and played with the gap between.

She caught her breath and her knees buckled slightly as more hands grasped her breasts.

Don't do this to me, one half of her mind shouted. The other half was intrigued, aroused and possibly even frightened.

Whoever stood in front of her placed one hand over her breast which it squeezed whilst playing with her nipple. The other hand slid down between her legs.

Something cold and soft dripped into the crease of her behind and into her anus. A finger followed.

Fingers played with the sensitive spot between her legs before going onwards to enter her vagina.

Lost in her own darkness, her very soul seemed to dance and spin in ecstasy, receiving all these sensations, yet hearing and seeing nothing. It was as though she were sex itself; a bit like an electrical transformer, taking everything in, storing it and changing it into something else, something personal and eminently solitary.

Lips brushed over her neck and breasts. Nipples were sucked into a warm, wet mouth.

Madness could result from this, Mariella thought as her mind attempted to rationalise the sensations she was receiving. Ecstasy was the only word to describe it.

She was vaguely aware of the sheik calling her back into his desert and the depths of her own decadent fantasies. This time she could not go.

The hands that had caressed her now took hold of her and laid her out on the floor. Instinctively, she knew it wasn't Peter's cock that entered her. There was a hint of coarseness about it, a thickness that was both alien and exciting.

His hands gripped her hips tightly and raised them as he pushed himself into her.

The other hands that had been on her buttocks were now on her breasts. The softness of inner thighs brushed against her cheeks. A smell that was both familiar and slightly worrying filled her nostrils before silky strands of pubic hair brushed her nose and mouth. Satin soft lips kissed her mouth, lips that parted to expose the labia and clitoris within.

There was no time for protest, no time to think that this was alien to her.

Too enraptured by what was happening, she willingly flicked out her tongue at the silky flesh, tasting its salty freshness, its slippery consistency.

Her hips began to rise of their own accord, thrusting with his thrust. Her tongue lapped at the seeping wetness, tasting the honeyed saltiness, rolling it around her mouth, taking it into her throat.

When she came, it was not as though they were people. It was merely as though they were implements, tools by which she had reached her own satisfaction.

Her darkness persisted until they too had finished, the thick penis spurting into her womb, the female riding a jerking spasm against her mouth.

When they had finished, they got her onto her knees and removed the ear muffs. Mariella trembled. Her body was covered in a fine layer of sweat, yet still she shivered with the after-effects of her orgasm.

A hand took hold of her chin. A woman laughed.

'She'll suit us well.'

'Well enough.'

Mariella turned her head in the direction of the male voice. She recognised it only as being foreign, but not someone she knew.

'Well? More than well, I can assure you,' she heard Peter say.

The other man grunted.

A hand caressed her shoulder. A soft female voice whispered, 'Yes.'

'Then we have a deal,' she heard Peter say. 'It has been a long day. Perhaps you will excuse me now.'

She heard them utter the usual things that people do after a dinner party or some such affair. Sounds of clothes being slid over bodies preceded the sound of the door opening and closing again.

Peter kissed her shoulder as he loosened the blindfold.

Blinking, Mariella looked up into his face. 'Who were they?' she demanded. 'What was this all about?'

Peter merely smiled. 'Now, now, my darling. Not so angry. I have merely negotiated a little deal for you. It is up to you whether you accept it or not.'

The fingers that caressed her face were very cold. So were the ones that untied her hands.

Mariella breathed heavily as a smiling Peter helped her to her feet. Her eyes blazed. Her mouth was set in a straight line.

'What deal? What are you talking about?'

Eyes still blazing, she rubbed at her wrists whilst he rubbed at her arms.

'That was van der Loste.'

'The Dutchman?'

Still rubbing her arms, Peter nodded. 'That's right. The other man who bid for my icon. I want you to go with him. I want you to find my icon, my darling.'

The lips that would have kissed her mouth landed in her hair as she angrily tossed her head.

'Joe Carey hasn't got the icon.' She looked at Peter sidelong. 'So it stands to reason that Hans does, so what's the point in me going with him?'

Peter kissed her mouth. This time she didn't turn away.

'To find out where he keeps it, my darling.'

Running his hands up and down her naked back, he hugged her to him.

'You will enjoy the experience,' he said in that low, grating voice of his. 'You will enjoy it very much.'

Feeling tired now, Mariella leaned more heavily on him, soothed by the warmth of his hands on her back.

Yet her mind was not with him, not tonight.

She was thinking of Etienne and meeting him at the café on Saturday night.

'When am I supposed to join him?' she murmured.

'Monday,' he replied.

Still hugging her naked body, he smiled into the darkness.

'Do not worry,' he added. 'Hans van der Loste is a man very much like myself. We have a great deal in common.'

Mariella closed her eyes. His voice poured over her like warm oil. There was comfort in the warmth of his body, but she did not see the deceit in his eyes.

From his high tower, Claude Doriere watched as the big Dutchman and his red-haired mistress left the hotel foyer. He did not need his telescope for this. He merely stood on his balcony and looked down as they stepped into their car.

Hans van der Loste was familiar to him. His mouth turned down at the thought of the man. An acrid, bitter taste sprang onto his tongue. His mind went back in time.

Cheats, thieves, and murderers. That was the best way in which to describe black marketeers and all the other people who made money just after the Revolution.

Hans van der Loste was one of those men, though he couldn't recall him being called that then.

All he could remember about him was the young girls to whom he offered jobs in places like Paris, Rome and Vienna.

'Parents, why let your daughters be caught up in the horrors of war? Spare them that. I can guarantee your daughters jobs in the city. They will be maids to fine ladies. Honest cooks in rich houses.' A big speech from a big man. That was van der Loste.

Claude gritted his teeth and locked his jaw. Horrible as it was to revive such memories, he forced himself to do it. Again he saw the big, placid face of the Dutchman a few years ago.

Claude thanked his lucky stars he had acquired a position as attendant on the only train left running from Moscow to Vienna. In those heady days after the Revolution, when red Russian was still fighting white and Lenin was laying the foundation for a modern nation, thousand upon thousand had fled their homeland. A thousand at a time, he used to think, had all piled on the train at once. That was how crowded it was.

Some people, of course, could afford their own cabin. One of these had been Hans van der Loste.

On a day crowded with people, and like all the others he had known since being an attendant, Claude had been allocated to the service of the big Dutchman who was a regular passenger on the train.

'More food,' the big man had regularly called out. 'More drink.'

Tray balanced on one hand, Claude had entered the cabin. The sight that met his eyes was completely unexpected, and him being a young man, it made him blush.

'I'm sorry,' he had exclaimed, his eyes wide with shocked surprise.

'Come forward,' ordered van der Loste as Claude started to retreat out of the door.

Trying his best to avert his eyes from the scene, Claude closed the door behind him and advanced to where Mr van der Loste was sitting.

'Put the drinks down on the table,' the Dutchman commanded.

Claude had done just that, his eyes still fixed on the floor.

Yet it was hard to be polite, to be demure. There were six girls in the cabin, all young, pale skinned and firm fleshed. They were naked and kneeling before the big man, eyes downcast. Each bottom was also criss-crossed with a mass of pink stripes. He thought he heard one of them sobbing.

'Shut up,' he heard van der Loste say as he eased himself

out of the door backwards. 'How can I get you a good position if you insist on blubbering all the time?'

Once the door was closed, Claude had leaned against it, his heart pounding in his chest, eyes half closed as he fought to come to terms with what he had seen.

'Slave labour,' he had muttered to himself. 'Those poor young girls.'

The girls had been locked in their cabins that night. Claude had let them out, told them to get well away and what their fate would most likely be if they did not.

'Will you go too?' they had asked.

He had shook his head. 'I can't. I must get to Paris. My mother is there.'

The following morning, all hell broke loose on the Moscow to Paris express.

Van der Loste thundered up and down the train, accusing everyone he came across of abducting his 'wards', girls whose parents had placed them under his protection.

'You!' shouted the Dutchman on spotting the cabin attendant who had brought in the drinks on the previous day. 'Did you set them free, you snivelling little Frenchman?'

The Dutchman had attempted to grab hold of his collar. Claude had side-stepped.

'Monsieur?'

At that point, one of the Dutchman's aides had called out and asked whether they should get off the train and go back the way they had come.

Claude had chosen that moment to disappear. As he did so, he had smiled to himself. The Dutchman had no doubt worked out that the girls would not have fled if they truly believed they were going to fill positions in great houses. Someone would have had to explain it to them, and in order to do that, they would have to speak Russian.

Claude's mother was French. His father had been Russian.

Chapter 22

Mariella knew an ending had occurred when she saw the look on Peter's face. She had just told him she was going out with a waiter she had met at a small café. A certain superiority came upon him that made him stand taller and hold his head that much higher. However, she had not expected him to appear quite so disdainful.

'Then go off with your little peasant.' His look was arrogant, his tone contemptuous.

Still with a haughty look on his noble features, he turned away.

'Aren't you going to wish me a good time?' she asked.

'I wish you all you wish yourself,' he responded with a backward glance over his shoulder. 'You know how I feel about consorting with the lower classes. I am therefore of the opinion that our relationship is at an end.'

He turned his back on her and walked to the table from where he took the morning newspaper.

Mariella felt a sudden pang of regret. After all, brushing three years aside was never likely to be easy. Was she really doing the right thing?

She reached out for him, the gesture uncertain. Should she touch him?

Peter made the decision for her. To her surprise, he took a step to avoid her reaching fingers.

His look was as chill as his voice. 'As I have just said, I wish you whatever you wish yourself. It is of no consequence to me if you wish to avail yourself of the services of the lower classes.'

She stared at him. Peter had always had his cruel moods, his sad moods, even his jealous moods. But never had she seen him so incredibly aloof.

Nothing like Valentino, she thought to herself, and wondered why she had ever thought so in the first place.

'Then I'll go.'

Frowning, she kept her eyes on him as she reached behind her for the door handle.

The chains that had bound her to him fell swiftly away. Once the door to his room was closed, so was that part of her life she had shared with him; a room she had once lived in, left behind. A new door was opening. A new room beckoned. Etienne awaited her, and she wanted to be with him.

Just as on the first night, the Café Nuit Noir was bubbling with life.

The night was mild, so the outside tables and chairs were full of babbling people.

A few young women in short, slinky dresses and cute little cloche hats were dancing in a line, arms linked so they looked like a battalion of multi-coloured tulips. There were a few older women dancing among them, their big backsides jiggling and their wide aprons bouncing as they kicked their legs in time with the music.

Face bright with happiness, Mariella made her way through the crowds. All the while, her eyes searched for Etienne, neck stretching, heart thumping with the desire to see him again.

She pushed her way through the dancing crowds. The bell above the café door jangled as she pushed her way in, then jangled some more as other revellers pushed their way out.

Slightly anxious, her gaze scoured the café for a sign of the slim waiter with the dark brown eyes.

Subject to the kind of homing mechanism inspired by sexual attraction and romantic affiliation, her eyes automatically went to the table in the alcove.

The chairs were unfilled, but a bottle of red wine and two glasses sat on the table.

Mariella hesitated. Was the wine really for her and Etienne? Or had it been left there by some other waiter whilst the customers danced through the shadows in the area through the archway?

Hesitant still, she made her way through the crowded bar. As she got nearer the table, she peered to where couples were cuddling close, striding wide as a tango belted out from the accordion.

'You came.'

She recognised his voice at once. She spun round. 'Etienne!'

She was aware she sounded breathless. She even felt breathless.

'Mariella.' He took both her hands in his. 'Come.'

He led her to the table, and again she sat in the tight space against the wall.

Once they were sitting, he raised her hand to his lips and kissed her palm. The gesture thrilled her. It was gentle, yet at the same time, it was also extremely erotic.

'I am so glad you came.' His dark eyes looked deeply into hers. One hand went to the wine bottle. He poured a measure into each glass.

'I have so much to tell you,' Mariella blurted suddenly.

He raised his eyebrows, but only smiled as if urging her to continue.

'I've decided to stay in St Asaph,' she said breathlessly. 'I am leaving my present lover.'

Still smiling, Etienne nodded slowly and she had a great urge to grab his chin and shower his face with kisses.

'Is this anything to do with me?' he asked.

'Yes . . . But . . .' Mariella found herself struggling for words. 'I don't really know what it is.' She leaned closer to him. Merely looking at the intensity of his eyes, the straightness of his nose, the firmness of his chin sent tremors of excitement racing through her body. Just looking at him made her think of someone else, someone who had dominated her life since she'd seen him in a picture house in Vienna.

'Why did you get involved with him in the first place?'

Taken aback by his question, she stared open mouthed and

thought she saw a hint of hardness come to Etienne's eyes.

She gestured with her hands; shrugged. 'I suppose . . .' She hesitated. Somehow she needed time to think and yet, deep down, she knew the reason very well. Did she have the courage to voice it?

When she eyed his face, it seemed all her secrets rushed to the surface. They'll all burst out like large boils over my skin if I don't confess, she thought. Then she sighed the sort of sigh that sounds like surrender. It was like that. She was surrendering to the truth.

'It was because of Valentino. Peter looks a bit like Valentino.'

Etienne raised one incredulous eyebrow. 'The American film star?'

Mariella nodded. 'Yes. I was young. I'd seen Rudolph Valentino in a film he'd acted in. It was called *The Sheik*. I couldn't get him out of my mind. He made me think things and want to do things I'd never done before. There was something about his eyes; something about his voice. Then Peter came along – just at the right time, I suppose. You might even say he swept me off my feet!'

Her laugh was low and hollow, and she had difficulty looking into Etienne's eyes. A faint blush came to her cheeks. She felt foolish.

'But he did more than that. He had exactly the same menace as Valentino did in the film. I was enthralled by him just as much as if I'd been seeing him up on the silver screen and me in the audience surrounded by all that darkness. That's the way it feels – or rather felt.'

'You don't feel like that any more?'

She found the confidence to look into his face again and shook her head. 'Don't get me wrong. He can still arouse me given the right circumstances.' She thought of the previous night. Of the Dutchman, of the woman. Until now she had not questioned their comments about her being right for their purposes. Even now she shrugged the statements aside, presuming them to be pre-written pieces designed specifically for Peter's amusement.

Eyes gazing into hers, Etienne raised her hand to his lips. 'Will you come with me tonight?'

She nodded. 'Yes.'

Without words passing between them, Mariella knew he was asking her to spend the whole night with him.

Shivering, she followed Etienne as he guided her through a damp tunnel that was carved out of solid rock and burrowed beneath the hotel in which she was staying.

'What is this place?' she asked. The question echoed off the cavern walls before Etienne answered.

'It leads up into the hotel. There used to be an abbey there at one time. According to local history, a lord who had a fine house in the town was in love with the abbess. There were already deep caverns within the rocks, but he extended them a little so he could visit his lady without anyone knowing about it. I have found his tunnel very useful.'

The tunnel steepened the nearer they got to the high rise of land where the hotel was situated.

Iron grated in an ancient lock as Etienne turned a huge key in a nail-studded door.

'This will take us to my private quarters,' he explained as he opened another door to a small, winding staircase.

The stairs were steep and made of stone. Up and up they circled, continually spiralling in on themselves, the climb as dizzying as it was breathless.

One more door, and the ancient staircase was left behind.

'This is my home,' he said at last. 'Would you care for a cocktail?'

Wide eyed, Mariella entered the room.

'This is yours?'

Etienne grinned warmly as he poured measures of brightly coloured liquid into thin-stemmed glasses.

'This is mine. I have to confess I do not make a living purely doing this.' He nodded at the two glasses he had just filled. 'I employ waiters. I do not need to work as one. I own this place. This hotel.'

Mariella took the glass he offered, glancing at the warm red liquid before taking in the details of a masculine place of sharp angles, cool colours, and clean lines. One article stood out from all the others.

'You watch the stars?' she asked, her fingers running gently over the shining brass of a large telescope.

'I watch a lot of things. I watched you from the first day you arrived. I also watched your lover.' His face darkened. 'He is someone I thought I would never see again.'

Mariella frowned. For the first time, she saw hatred in Etienne's eyes. 'You know Peter?'

'It was a long while ago. Come. Let me show you the stars.'

His dismissal was obvious, yet Mariella allowed him to take hold of her shoulders as he manoeuvred both the telescope and her body into the right place for stargazing.

'You look through here,' he said showing her the brass-rimmed eye piece.

He raised the viewing lens until she could see through it. With a flash of brilliant light, the whole solar system seemed to be within touching distance. It was impossible not to marvel at the stunning brightness of it all, the fact that distances were immense, yet brought down to size by a series of magnifying devices.

'I never knew how marvellous it could be,' Mariella murmured, her gaze still fixed on the heavens.

Etienne rested his hand upon her waist. 'Do you really like it?'

Mariella straightened up and looked at him. 'I think it's a real treasure, and not because it is simply beautiful to look at.'

He looked satisfied. He also looked as though he were fighting to reach a decision. Eventually he came to it.

'Come,' he said, offering her his hand as he had before. 'Let me show you my other treasures.'

Gleaming with starlight, the room he took her to was a place with dark blue tiled floors. The stars themselves seemed to form the roof and walls, though the truth was that the whole room was constructed of glass.

Renaissance paintings sat on dark wooden easels. Sculpted marble figures wrestled or posed beneath the night time sky. A single icon rested on an ebony easel. Nearby sat a death mask cast in gold and belonging to the Aztec nation rather than the Egyptian.

Mariella's eyes went over the objects again and again. But one object struck her above all others. The very look of it was in her mind, and yet she had to look again, to see for sure that it was what she suspected.

'This icon,' she said as she stood before it. 'Have you had it long?'

Etienne came up and stood behind her. He rested his hands on her shoulders and planted a kiss in her hair.

'I stole it.'

Mariella swallowed the urge to look surprised.

'Who from?'

'A man who stole it from the church. A man I should have killed while I had the chance.'

Somehow, Mariella was under no doubt as to who he meant. No matter what story Peter had told her, she suddenly knew he'd been lying.

Without her urging him to, Etienne began to tell her the true story.

'It was 1922. Red and white Russians were still fighting, but it was obvious that Lenin had consolidated his position. The stronger he got, the more those opposed to his principles poured out of the country. Of course, those opposed to his principles sometimes had a lot more to lose than their lives. The wealthy fled in droves, their valuables safe in some secret bank account.

'Even so, there were some people who took advantage of the chaos and stole other things on the way. The icon was one of those things.

'The man who stole it had coveted it for a long time. When the chance came, he took it. I heard of his intention and tried to stop him.'

'But what were you doing in Russia?' Mariella asked as they settled themselves onto a comfortable grey velvet settee.

'I was visiting my father. He was Russian, you see. My mother was French, his mistress, not his wife. That is why I use the name Claude Doriere. It was my mother's father's name. I prefer to use the name Etienne which is my true name.'

Mariella nodded but said nothing. He had captured her interest. She wanted to hear more.

Etienne hugged her close. As he spoke he squeezed her hand. His gaze settled somewhere on the floor about two feet away from the settee.

'My father was dying, but he begged me before he went to go after my half-brother. He knew his intention was to steal the icon. My brother was like a magpie, you see. He loved shiny things, especially if they had some erotic history.

'So I went after him. The snow was deep outside the church and I could see his footsteps. I stood in the middle of the path waiting for him to come out. When he did, he snarled at me. Even though he barely knew me and my face was wrapped around with furs, he knew by my eyes who I was. He shouted at me to go back to France, to my mother who was no better than a whore.

'That in itself was enough to make me angry. I lunged at him. In the streets of Paris I had learned to use a knife. I went nowhere without it.

'My brother came for me with a long dagger. But I was quicker than he was. I lashed out, and as I did so, I grabbed the icon.

'The last I saw of him, his blood was staining the snow.'

'And the icon? You didn't return it?'

Mariella's eyes were as big as saucers, fascinated, but not without a sign of resentment towards him.

Etienne smiled. 'Yes. I did return it. Catherine the Great gave it to the church, and that's where it should be. But first I had a copy made. That is the one you see in there. The church rewarded me which enabled me to buy this hotel.'

Leaning forward, he rested his elbows on his knees, his head in his hands. Mariella began to rub his back.

'You know,' she heard him say, 'the very first day I saw you, I saw him too. I'd know that bastard half-brother of mine anywhere. I also saw the scar on his face. Count Peter Stavorsky. My brother!' He slowly turned his head and looked at her over his shoulder. 'And my rival.'

Mariella draped herself around his shoulders. 'He's been looking for that icon.' She felt his hair against her lips as she spoke. 'He's desperate to find it. That's why he had me make contact with Joe Carey, the American. He thought he had it.'

Etienne straightened and looked at her. 'Did he, now? That is very interesting.

'I shall explain,' he said on seeing Mariella's puzzled expression. 'I made a promise to the church that I would cover my tracks well so that Peter would not seek out their icon again. Naively, I presumed that if he heard it was in the possession of some wealthy patron, he would forget about it. Obviously I was wrong.'

Thoughtfully, Mariella caressed Etienne's cheek. 'But he doesn't know you have the icon – albeit a copy. And he doesn't know who you are. He certainly wouldn't be staying in your hotel if he did.'

Etienne's eyelids flickered and there was a questioning look in his eyes. 'But once he does, he might come after me. Is that what you're hinting at?'

The look Mariella gave him was enough confirmation that it was.

'You could be in danger.'

'I could.'

'So we should do something about it.'

Their eyes met in mute understanding.

'I have to give him the copy. But how? I can hardly face him and say, "Here you are, Peter. Have this icon. Sorry about slashing your face."'

'You don't need to.'

Mariella's look was suddenly as bright as her voice.

'I know someone who's said he'll do anything for me. He's shortly going to be taken at his word.'

'Will you tell me who it is?'

Smiling, Mariella wrapped her arm about his neck so she could bring his face closer to hers.

'No,' she whispered. 'Not yet. Perhaps in the morning.'

No sheik appeared to add extra verve to Mariella's arousal. On the grey satin sheets of Etienne's bed, there were only two bodies, and it was the same in Mariella's mind. Their flesh moved as one, their ardour hot and burning. Needles of sensation seared through her nipples, ignited by the ministrations of Etienne's fingers.

The warmth of his palms made her stomach muscles spasm, the prodding of his penis made her sex juicy with apprehension, made her mind long for him to invade her body.

He entered, and both came, but their lovemaking did not stop at one climax only. Satisfaction lasted for only minutes before their ardour resurfaced.

His mouth traced down where his hand had gone earlier. His lips sucked on her pubic hair, his tongue dipped between her pubic lips, the dew of her desire lying like nectar on his tongue.

Moaning with delight, she caressed his thighs. As though it was some hidden message, he turned his body so that his thighs were over her face, his penis gently tapping at her lips.

As she tasted him, she closed her eyes. Yet there was no Valentino to use her body. No fantasy intruded into reality. Etienne was real. She was real, and so was the passion that boiled between them.

In the morning, they set out their plan.

'First,' said Mariella. 'I will go and see Joe.'

'And I will watch,' stated Etienne.

'And I will play my part,' Mariella returned. 'Just like a movie star.'

Chapter 23

Joe looked pleased to see her.

'Would you like tea?' he asked.

Mariella was instantly reminded of the first time they had taken tea together. On that occasion the taste of Peter in her mouth had mingled with the taste of the tea.

After setting down her parcel, she shook her head. 'No thanks.'

They sat in the blue-striped chairs set out on the saloon deck.

'Anything else I can get you?' Joe asked, his face intense, his voice enthusiastic.

Mariella lowered her eyes and clasped her hands around her knees.

'Do you recall our day in Marseilles?'

A bright red flush came over Joe's face before he nodded.

'Oh yes!'

'And you recall our little adventure on the beach.'

'Oh yes!'

She raised her eyes to meet his.

'Do you also recall promising you'd do anything to help me should I need help?'

'I did.'

'I need your help now. A simple task, really, but one for which I would be very grateful.'

'Anything!'

His eyes were bright and very round. His bright white teeth showed from between his open lips.

Mariella reached for the parcel. She brought it onto her

lap and sat it there, her fingers tapping against it thoughtfully as though she were deciding whether to unwrap it or not.

Adopting a helpless look, she gazed into his eyes.

'You know I have a lover, don't you, Joe?'

Joe stared. The bright expression was not so bright.

'I want to leave him, Joe, but there's a problem. He's likely to follow me unless he recovers something he covets much more than me.'

Joe's eyes dropped to the parcel. Mariella's fingers were curving over the string that bound the brown paper.

'This object I have here in my lap is very valuable to him. This is the object he covets more than he does me. I have to get it to him. The problem is, I don't want him to ask where it came from. That is where you come in.'

Joe's face relaxed, yet a keenness came to his eyes, the sharpness born of being brought up in the wrong spot in the wrong city and of the wrong kind of parentage.

'Go on,' he said slowly.

Mariella caught the more calculating look in his eyes, and although it unnerved her, she chanced it held no threat.

'He knows you have a collection of icons that you wish to sell. He knows you do not have it in your museum at Marseilles, or at least he knows you never showed it to me.'

'How does he know?'

There was no mistaking Joe's look of accusation.

The wronged woman took over. 'I'm sorry, Joe.' Her head sank into her hands. 'You don't know what sort of man he is. He's cruel. Perverted. I had to do it.' She reached for his hand. He tensed, but did not retreat.

'Joe, will you approach him? Will you offer him the icon as if it had always been in your possession? This icon?' The brown paper crackled as she patted it.

Joe looked from her to the package.

'What if he asks how I knew he wanted it?'

'Tell him I confessed.'

Joe blinked. He stared at her, then glanced at the package.

His gaze went back to her before he sighed. There was no doubting the resignation in the deeply exhaled breath. 'Show me,' he said.

Fingers sure, Mariella undid the package. Gold glittered in the sunlight, rubies flashed like drops of frozen blood, emeralds like chips of frozen sea. Glistening as though wet, a blue-robed Madonna raised one hand in blessing.

'It's beautiful,' Joe remarked, his fingers tracing the carved forms that made up the gold frame. 'Not that icons are to my particular taste, as I told you.'

Mariella retained her air of helplessness, though inside she was tense with apprehension. There was no guarantee that Joe would help her; no guarantee that the plan would work.

At last Joe looked at her and smiled. 'All right. I'll do it. Where is this lover of yours?'

'Room 408. Hotel le Grande Sophie. His room has a telephone.'

'My boat does not,' Joe quipped. They both laughed.

But Joe stopped laughing. A thoughtful look came to his eyes.

Mariella tensed. Wire wool seemed to knot up in her stomach.

'I have to make a condition,' he said. His eyes seemed to glitter. Mariella felt suddenly very naked, very vulnerable.

She made the effort and succeeded in keeping her voice even.

'What condition is that?'

'I'd like you to order me to do it. Just like you did in Marseilles.'

Earlier that day, Mariella had told Etienne that such a condition was likely.

'I understand,' he'd said, his words muted against her hair, his hands warm upon her bare back. He'd kissed her forehead, her nose, her lips. 'Do what you have to do. Our future together depends on it.'

Etienne's words in her mind, Mariella rose from her chair.

'What about your crew? We need privacy.'

'That's no problem. I'll order them to set sail, plot a course, then go down below. We'll have the deck to ourselves.'

True to her part, Mariella's smile faded. A hard glint came to her eyes. 'What are you waiting for? Do it! Do it now!'

Joe jumped to it.

She could tell by the speed at which he was barking orders that his balls were probably heavy with anticipation and his cock hard with expectations.

The engine swerved them away from the dock and out into open water. Once the sea was judged deep enough, the sails were unfurled and a course set. The crew melted away like early morning mist.

Mariella tilted her head back and looked at the great white sails against the bright blue of the sky. Slivers of white that were seagulls' wings soared far above the mast.

'Is this safe?' she asked Joe.

'Perfectly safe. The course has been set and the rudder fixed in that position.'

She saw his jaw tremble as he looked at her. 'We're alone. I'm all yours.'

A slow smile came to her face. It widened as she danced her fingers over the crisp, white shirt he was wearing.

But light-heartedness was not what Joe wanted. Mariella set her jaw firm, her eyes hard.

She curled her fingers around the front edges of his so neat shirt. With one mighty effort, she ripped the two edges apart. He gasped. She almost drooled as the firm, bronzed beauty of his chest was exposed to her view.

But she was not here to show her approval of him, only her dominance.

However, she could not resist biting his nipples.

He cried out. He moaned, and she became excited.

Aroused by her own actions, she brought all the power of her imagination to bear on what she would do to him next.

Ripping his shirt down to his elbows, she gathered the tails and pulled him towards the main mast. Once there, she pulled his shirt behind him. She heard him gasp with pleasure as she tied his wrists together.

'I'm going to tie you up with your own ropes,' she murmured.

He trembled. He moaned, but he did not protest either in words or in action.

Turning him so he faced the mast, she bound a rough rope around his upper torso and did it so that his elbows were bent and his wrists caught beneath it.

Hands on hips, she stood back to admire her handiwork.

'You look good,' she commented as she eyed his straining arm muscles, his prominent shoulder blades. 'In fact, you look just the way I want you to look. Vulnerable. Weak. Entirely at my mercy, as all men should be.'

One finger tapped thoughtfully at her chin as she considered her next move.

Her hands went around to the front of Joe's trousers. She undid the buttons, then pulled both his trousers and underwear to his ankles.

The sight of his bare buttocks caused a severe tingling to occur between her legs. Even her nipples throbbed against her camisole, though heaven knows, the silk was soft enough.

Eyes shining, tongue licking away the dryness of her lips, she slipped her hand beneath his buttocks and gently squeezed his hanging sac.

Joe moaned, a mixture of ecstasy and agony as his legs parted.

Mariella took a deep intake of breath as she ran her hands over Joe's buttocks. She pressed herself against him, arms around him as she sniffed at his skin, kissing it in places, her own desire becoming something like torture.

Shivers of delight swept over Joe's body. But was all his body so thrilled with her actions?

Mariella slid her hands around his hips and down into his loins. Her fingers touched the velvet-sheathed hardness of his erection. The tip of his penis was touched with a slippery, warm wetness. His whole stem rocked gently, then pulsed as she wrapped her fingers around it.

Devious schemes came to her mind. Even Valentino returned to inspire her with his menacing looks and perverted ways.

Make him come, he ordered. But not in the way he would like to.

Yes, decided Mariella. Yes! That is exactly what I will do. In that, there was power. In that there was satisfaction.

He cried out as she pulled on his prick so its tip almost reached his belly. Then she pushed him flat against the gnarled ropes that ran around the mast. His member was trapped, the abrasiveness of the ropes rough against his aching rod.

She wound another rope around his waist, another around the top of his thighs.

She heard him whimper at the itching roughness of the sisal fibres.

'That's it,' she exclaimed, her mouth close to his face. 'That's it. I love to hear you groan because then I can imagine how painful it must be to have your cock rub against the rope. But,' she added, 'I have not finished yet.'

Rope, she discovered, was plentiful on a sailing yacht. She found a particularly splendid piece that was ideal for her purposes, being about three feet in length and knotted at one end.

Excitement made her face turn pink. Her fingers curled and uncurled around the piece of rope as she contemplated where she should let the first blow land.

Get on with it, ordered a voice in her head. She knew who it was, of course.

'I thought you'd left me,' she whispered softly.

Beat him, snarled the voice. Let's see how pink you can make that firm backside of his!

Heart beating fast, blood rushing, Mariella raised her length of rope and let it fall, whistling through the air, to land with a loud crack on Joe's buttocks.

'No!' he screamed.

He means yes, urged the voice in Mariella's head.

'Yes!' she repeated.

Again she raised her arm, and again the rope flew through the air to leave another red mark on Joe's behind.

'Yes,' she said again. 'Yes! Yes! Yes!'

Each time she said that small word, the rope rose and fell, rose and fell. Each time, Joe pressed himself more tightly against the mast trying, as if he could, to escape the blows that rained upon his flesh.

Each time, Joe cried out, though the sounds weakened until they were no more than whimpers.

Face pink, eyes glittering with excitement, Mariella at last dropped the piece of rope and stared at her handiwork.

Joe's gloriously firm behind was criss-crossed with dark pink stripes.

She felt a stirring in her groin looking at them; felt a strong urge to touch them.

Gently, with only her fingertips, she touched the pink stripes.

Joe groaned and shivered as her fingers traced the result of her beating. His flesh was reassuringly hot beneath her touch, and the sight of it thrilled her.

Like a wild butterfly, beating its wings against glass, her breath fluttered in her throat. Eyes shining, she clasped her throat as if that would help her breathe more evenly. The effort was hopeless. Doing this to such a man was new to her. Doing this to *any* man was new to her. Even in her fantasies, it had always been her submitting, her being subjected to the more refined forms of torture that aroused rather than repelled the subject.

But here she was, not the subject, not the submissive, but the dominator. The sheik.

A shiver passed through her. Moist lips parted as she panted with sheer lust.

Because she had imagined such scenarios a thousand times

over, she instinctively knew how he was feeling; she could easily imagine the coarseness of the sisal ropes against his trapped member.

The thought was delicious, and being such, one thought led to another.

She went to him, ran her hands down his back, her fingernails over his abused flesh.

His moan turned to a low whimpering as she slid her hand between his legs and squeezed the softness of his scrotal sac.

'Are you still my slave?' she asked softly between sweet kisses. 'Do you truly worship me as you should?'

'Yes . . .'

His voice was weak with emotion.

Mariella smiled to herself. Half closing her eyes, she sighed, breathed in his smell, and rubbed her body against him until he could not help but thrust himself against the mast and the heavy ropes wound around him.

'Then I will ride you,' she whispered. 'Just as I rode you on the marble floor of the museum.'

As she stood back and began to strip her clothes from her body, she looked at him, her own flesh alive with excitement. The ache between her legs grew stronger as she viewed his body glistening with sweat, his muscles trembling with intermittent tension.

Once she was stripped down to only her stockings and her shoes, she approached him, her breath racing, breasts heaving in anticipation.

Snuggling up against him, she rested her naked breasts on his hands and mewed with satisfaction as his fingers curled around them.

She held his shoulders so that her body was pressed tightly against his. Once her pubes were against his buttocks, she began to jerk, her legs slightly open so she could get the full benefit of his firm flesh on her clitoris.

With each thud of her hips against his, Joe's own pelvis rammed against the rough rope, and even though he made noises that loitered between agony and ecstasy, his fingers did lovely things to her nipples.

Mariella was slowly losing herself in her own sensations. Her breasts were tantalised by his hands, her sex was enlivened by the thud of her clitoris against his flesh.

Throwing back her head, she closed her eyes, opened her mouth and let her cries go free.

In her mind she was riding naked across a vast expanse of sand, her sex aroused by the movement of the horse and the leather of the saddle.

Her mind swayed between fantasy and reality, between a leather saddle and the feel of Joe's flesh. And the way her nipples felt, how could only a breeze be eliciting such delight? It was Joe's hands doing this to her, Joe whose desires were close to her own.

When she came, she shuddered against him, her legs trembling, her pelvis ramming fiercely, then clamping herself to him as her climax rushed out from her loins.

Muscles quivering, Joe cried out, his own pelvis mating with the rope, the masthead and the stickiness of his own ejaculation which christened the ropes and seeped over his belly.

The fantasy horse stood still in Mariella's mind. Her race was run. The desert itself faded away, and as she opened her eyes, she saw the back of Joe's neck, his soaked hair, and the sweat that lay between his nose and his lip.

Lightly, her lips grazed his back and her tongue tasted the saltiness of his skin.

'The icon?'

It was all she needed to say.

Slowly, as if in a mute act of submission, Joe closed his eyes, then, just as slowly opened them again.

'Yes,' he murmured. 'The icon.'

Chapter 24

The night being warm and Mariella being pleased with herself, she decided to stroll along the quay back to the hotel.

The icon had been left in Joe's safekeeping and she had no reason to suppose he would not adhere to her wishes.

Light fell in a broad expanse from café windows, or in small squares from one of the few remaining fisherman's cottages that still clung like limpets to the edge of the quay.

Most catering premises had shut, the night given over to clubs where couples could dance to a band, or drink oddly named drinks made from even odder ingredients.

A few people walked by. A few cars glided on their way from nightclub to hotel, private villa to private yacht.

The air of St Asaph, the little fishing town that had slept like the Sleeping Beauty, smelt of youth, spring and the surging of the sea. As the clock on the church spire struck three, it suddenly seemed as if she were completely alone with only the sea and the night for company. No more people walked by, nor did any cars pass.

The purring of a car engine was not unusual, so Mariella did not turn round as a leather-bound running board passed close to her leg.

'Excuse me. Can you help us?'

It was a female voice addressing her, so she had no need to be afraid.

She turned round, vaguely aware that the voice was familiar. The woman's face was not. She had red hair and a wide smile.

'I am so sorry. I hope I did not frighten you at this hour of the night. But you see, we are lost.'

The woman got out of the car. The man sitting beside her

got out too. There was definitely something familiar about him, but the lights along the quay had gone out, so it was hard to bring his identity to mind.

'We are lost,' the woman repeated again.

Just as Mariella was about to answer, her arms were grabbed from behind.

The chauffeur!

As she was about to scream, a hand was clamped over her mouth, and her ankles were grabbed by the man who was vaguely familiar.

Struggling for all she was worth, she became aware that there was a greater darkness above her than night time. As she was bundled into a dark hole, she realised it was the boot of the car.

'Bind her tightly,' ordered a male voice. 'And gag her.'

'Did you bring something to gag her with?'

Mariella recognised the woman's voice.

'Use these!' exclaimed the man.

Rough hands ripped Mariella's cami-knickers from her body. Quickly, so as not to permit her to emit any sound at all, the knickers were tied around her mouth.

She felt her ankles as well as her wrists being tied. She wriggled, then jumped as a large hand slapped her naked bottom.

'Less of that!'

The chauffeur, with a care for her modesty, pulled her dress down over her naked loins.

The woman pushed him away.

'Leave her with something to think about!' The woman pulled the dress up until it was around Mariella's waist. The woman smiled. 'It will give us something to think about too.'

She kissed the man beside her. He smiled at her, then he looked down at Mariella. She cringed and did her best to get away from him.

But there was nowhere to go. Nothing she could do.

He ran his hand down her leg then let his fingers dally with her pubic hair. He tutted. 'Awful stuff. We will have this off as soon as possible.'

With that, the boot lid was pulled down and Mariella was plunged into total darkness.

The car moved off across the cobbles. She only knew they had been left behind once her ride became smoother, her body no longer being bumped up and down due to the uneven surface.

Eventually the car came to a halt, and with as much struggling and as little gentleness as before, she was bundled out of the car and thrown over the shoulder of the chauffeur.

Water lapped against the quay as she was taken onto a large motor yacht. She saw the man and the woman walking on behind.

What do they want with me? a voice in her head screamed.

Eyes wide with fear, she tried to turn her head, to call out in the direction of Joe's boat, *Stanza,* but the effort was wasted.

'Leave us,' snapped the woman once the chauffeur had flung her onto a narrow bunk in a small cabin.

As the door closed, Mariella stared up at the woman and the man who stood behind her.

Unsmiling, the woman reached down and jerked her skirt up so that her lower body was exposed.

'Shall I make a start right away?' she woman asked, her glance alternating between Mariella's sex and the man's face.

'Right away,' he replied. 'You know I like things neat and clean cut. Get rid of it.'

In the darkness, Mariella had not been sure of the man's identity. On seeing him in the light of the cabin, she recognised Hans van der Loste, the diamond dealer, the other man who might have had the Russian icon.

Smiling, his woman accomplice sat next to her on the bed.

Mariella lay still until the gag was removed.

'What the hell's going on?' she shouted, shifting her body abruptly so that her knees banged against the woman's hip.

'Please! Please!' trilled the woman, half closing her eyes and throwing her hands up before her face. 'We knew you might be annoyed at first. The count said you would.'

'Oh, did he!'

Mariella's eyes blazed and she wrenched her wrists, twisting them against her bonds.

The woman with the Titian hair went on unperturbed, her face placid, yet oddly provocative.

'He said that once things were explained to you, everything would be fine.'

Mariella jerked her head away as the woman attempted to stroke her hair.

'Why should it be fine? Would you be fine after being bundled into a car boot and being gagged with your own knickers?'

The woman made a comic face, raising her eyebrows and hiding a grin.

It suddenly came to Mariella just how funny it sounded. 'This is ridiculous.' She shook her head and managed a pretty sardonic smile. 'What the hell is going on? Get on, woman, and explain it to me.'

'Well,' said the woman, folding her hands in her lap. 'A few evenings ago the count was a guest on this boat. Whilst here he admired an icon that Hans has in his possession. He told us how he had lost one himself. It was agreed he buy it on the proviso that payment was made both in money and in kind. The kind was you. He said you would not mind. Is that not true?'

Mariella hesitated before replying. The boat was moving. She could feel the engines thumping below her, their power provided by a modern diesel engine.

'Where are we going?' she asked.

'Hans has an island. We're staying there for a few days while you pay off your debt.'

Mariella glared. 'You mean the count's debt!'

The woman nodded. 'The count's debt.'

Mariella thought quickly. 'And then I will be free to go?'

'Of course,' the woman said brightly. 'You may go wherever

you please. The count said so. He said he had other business to attend to. Apparently he is still searching for the icon that was stolen from him.'

Mariella lowered her eyes as she did some quick calculations. In a few hours' time Joe would be offering the copy of the icon provided by Etienne to Peter. This one he had bought from the diamond merchant was purely a sop in comparison to the one bequeathed to the church by Catherine the Great, the Scarlet Empress.

But would Peter swallow Joe's story about her not telling him the truth when she said Joe didn't have the icon?

Somehow, she decided, it might be better that she was out of the way until the deal was done and Peter was gone – as she was sure he would be by the time she got back.

'I see,' she muttered, her arms and legs relaxing against their constraints. 'Then I'd better conform to what's been agreed.' She threw in a convincing sigh.

A happy expression spread across the face of the woman with the red hair. 'Good!' she exclaimed. 'Good! Now then, Mariella, first I will tell you that my name is Tanya, and secondly I will tell you that I have to shave that off.'

One ringed finger pointed directly at Mariella's pubic thatch.

'Do you have to?'

Mouth turned down in a clownish fashion, Tanya nodded. 'I am afraid so. Hans' preference is for a shorn pussy, not one as profuse as the Black Forest.'

She laughed.

Mariella smiled, but inwardly groaned. Defoliation was not something that appealed to her. But in all honesty, at this moment in time she had no choice.

She sighed. 'All right. Start pruning.'

'Not here,' said Tanya, her fingers now busily untying the bonds around Mariella's ankles. 'I have a special room.'

Once she had also released Mariella's wrists, Tanya led her along the companionway.

The room they entered was crisply white. White cupboards

lined the walls and a white table sat in the middle of the room. A metal trolley sat beside it, rolling slightly on its rubber wheels as the boat hit choppy sea. It had the appearance of having escaped from a hospital, and with a wariness of the sea, to be attempting to get back there.

'Pull your dress up to your waist and get up on there,' Tanya ordered in an affable but firm way. She pointed to the white table which was at least seven feet long.

Mariella did as she was told, gasping as the coldness of the table met the warmth of her backside.

'Give me your hand, Mariella.'

Tanya took hold of her wrist. 'This is just to make sure you do not move. I do not want to cut you.'

A thick strap was wound around her wrist. A heavy metal buckle was fastened in some way to the side of her head. Tanya did the same with her other hand.

'And now,' exclaimed Tanya with a smile, 'we will make sure you cannot kick me.'

Mariella watched the mop of red hair go down then come back up again. There was a pole attached to the side of the table with a loop at one end.

An apprehensive shiver ran through Mariella's body as her other leg was also bent and raised, her ankle resting in the stirrup.

'There!'

Tanya looked pleased with herself, standing between the raised legs.

Mariella blushed. Never in either reality or fantasy had she been in such a vulnerable position, and never had a woman looked at her sex with such a lustful gaze.

She gritted her teeth and closed her eyes.

'Get it over with,' she muttered.

Tanya's touch was gentle, and the shaving lather was cool upon her pubic lips.

Tanya hummed while she worked, and only spoke when each delicate stroke was finished.

'Where did you meet the count?'

'In Vienna. I was at finishing school there.'

'I take it he swept you off your feet.' She carried out a sweeping arm movement as she removed yet another inch of soft, fair hair.

Mariella swallowed and tried not to look at what Tanya was doing.

'I suppose he did. I fell for it, anyway.'

Tanya hummed again and slid her fingers beneath one pubic lip while the other hand slid the razor through her hair.

'I can understand it,' said Tanya as she flung yet another tuft of hair into a bowl. 'After all, he is very handsome in a menacing, dark kind of way. In fact, he reminds me of that Hollywood film star. You know. The one in that film in the desert.'

Mariella murmured her reply. 'Yes. It was called *The Sheik*. He was called Rudolph Valentino.'

'That's right,' exclaimed Tanya with a final flourish of her hand. 'And that's the lot.'

Smiling directly at Mariella, she flattened her hand over Mariella's naked sex. Surprisingly enough, the warmth of Tanya's hand was welcome now that she no longer had any pubic hair to keep her warm.

But Mariella could see by the look in Tanya's eyes that there was more to her action that pure comfort.

'Does it feel good?' Tanya asked, her eyes gleaming.

Mariella opened her mouth to protest. Nothing came out except a sudden gasp.

Because her legs were so wide and her flesh so exposed, Tanya's palm felt pleasant against her clitoris and all the pale pink petals that surrounded it.

Despite the helplessness of her predicament, Mariella could not help but appreciate the very unique details.

Never had her sex felt so tantalised. Was this purely caused by the effect of having no pubic hair, or was it the fact that it was a woman's hand giving her pleasure?

'Do you like that?' Tanya asked as she squeezed the soft lips of Mariella's sex until she moaned, threw back her head and thrust out her breasts.

It was impossible not to arch her back as Tanya's thumb did little heartbeat presses against her clitoris. It was even more impossible not to cry out with ecstasy as two fingers entered her vagina.

'I shall be the first to make you come now you have lost your fur,' murmured Tanya, her eyes glowing like burning coals as she watched the object of her attention writhing and undulating against the hard table top. 'There,' she exclaimed, her voice hushed and breathless. 'Is that good? Is that not better than any man can do?'

Wet with desire and hot with a rising climax, Mariella found it impossible to find her voice. Something in her wanted to retreat from this experience, but something else in her wanted her to stay, to elicit as much pleasure out of it as possible.

In an attempt to retreat, she tried to hide herself in one of her desert fantasies; she wanted to tell herself that it was the sheik doing this, but the speed of her arousal and subsequent climax did not allow her the time.

Only in one rushed moment did she glimpse his eyes. But her climax dragged her away from him, and as it did so, she thought she saw something other than menace in his eyes. For the first time ever, she saw sadness, and although she reached for him, she could not touch him. Suddenly, the object of her sexual fantasies seemed no more the man he used to be. The vision dressed in black was fading and something within her seemed to fade with him.

Chapter 25

'I must ask you to wear this dress and these shoes?'

'That's no problem.' And it certainly wasn't. Haute couture was something Mariella had always appreciated. If clothes maketh the man, it certainly did a lot more than that for a woman. But the white dress Tanya indicated was something more than the product of an imaginative Parisian designer. It was rich in ornamentation, slinky and shiny, a full length sheath low at both the back and the front.

At first she presumed the glittering cascade of shininess that covered it to be chips of glinting glass. How could she be so wrong? She gulped once she'd reminded herself that Hans van der Loste was a diamond merchant.

'Do you like it?' asked Tanya, fearing Mariella's silence might signal non-compliance.

'I should think I do.' Mariella choked back the fact that she was considerably impressed.

'I will help you with it,' Tanya stated, pursing her dark red lips so that her pronounced cheeks seemed even rounder than they were.

Mariella, smelling sweet after a bath, was dressed in a white satin kimono which she had to continuously clasp around herself because the garment did not appear to have any fastening. She let it fall to the floor and prepared to step into the weighty looking dress rather than chance sliding it over her head.

'No expense spared,' Mariella murmured as the weight of the dress slid over her body. The rose diamonds sparkled as she moved and sent reflected light dancing around the cabin.

Mariella ran her hands down over the dress, the diamonds hard and cold beneath her touch. As she did so, a thrill ran through her body. The lining of the dress was obviously silk.

Normally, the feel of silk itself is an aphrodisiac, its cool lightness teasing the most sensitive, the most erogenous zones. But this dress did more than that. Because it was so encrusted with precious stones, it was heavy, and because it was heavy, it pressed the silk more consistently, more intently against her skin. Shivers ran over her flesh. It was as though her body too had a silk lining – no – a covering, a shivering coolness that ran between her skin and the silk.

The shoes that Tanya strapped on her feet were very high and fastened around the ankles with gold chains.

'I also have this for you,' giggled Tanya and for the moment sounded very much as if she were only lately out of school.

As if, thought Mariella, raising one eyebrow as she eyed Tanya's wide backside, small waist and full breasts. And if you ever did go to school, I bet biology was your favourite subject!

The thought did little to lift her spirits. Now she was here, she would have to go through whatever was planned for her. That was the deal Peter had made with this man, and in order to stop him looking for another icon and perhaps discovering Etienne, she had to go along with it. Hopefully, Joe would have convinced him of the authenticity of the icon by the time she got back. Then Peter would go and she would have Etienne all to herself.

Thinking about him made her wonder a little glumly whether he would miss her; whether he would come looking for her.

'Do you like it?' Tanya's husky voice broke into her thoughts.

Mariella blinked. 'What?'

'This! This!'

Tanya's voice had now adopted a hissing quality; like a snake; a very fat snake.

Mariella glanced to where an example of the very latest fashion item was displayed on a wax head. Skull caps were all the rage, quite the thing to wear with slinky evening dresses with scooped backs. Divine if the wearer was a sophisticated smoker complete with ebony cigarette holder.

'I don't smoke,' said Mariella vaguely as she bent forward in order to examine the cap more closely.

'Baby!' exclaimed Tanya, shrugging her shoulders and spreading her palms. 'You do not need to smoke to wear a cap like this. The thing is dripping with diamonds!'

Mariella didn't need to be told that. The cap begged attention, blazed in her face. The base was white but almost indistinguishable beneath the silver threads from which hung droplets of diamonds, like melting icicles. She could almost believe she would see water drip off them at any moment.

'Then if the cap fits . . .' exclaimed Mariella as she plumped herself down before the small fitted dressing table on which the item sat.

'Let me do it.'

Tanya's hands were on the cap before Mariella's.

'If you must.'

Mariella raised her eyes to the cap that hovered just above her head. Her gaze transferred to the mirror where she saw herself, the cap, and the gleaming face of the red-haired Tanya.

'Brush your hair back.'

Mariella did as she said.

Gently, Tanya fitted the cap over her head, her fingers smoothing the last vestiges of hair away from her face.

Mariella stared at her reflection. Her eyes looked bluer; bigger. Her lips looked perfectly formed, perfectly pink, and her cheekbones looked more chiselled than when they were framed with only a blonde bob.

'Is it not lovely?' Tanya sighed. Like an angel – a fallen one – she held her hands together as if about to spout an appropriate prayer.

'It's lovely.' Mariella nodded as she spoke which caused the hanging diamonds to tinkle like a peal of fairy bells.

If Tanya had been a little more observant, she would have

noticed the concern in Mariella's eyes. What was this all about? Why the beautiful dress, the beautiful skull cap? The cap itself must be worth a fortune. And the dress? Priceless. What did Hans van der Loste want from her?

But Mariella guessed that Tanya was a woman whose needs were simple. Men were men and sex was sex, and whatever a man wanted, she did her utmost to give.

Would that she was that uncomplicated! If only her mind was devoid of an imagination that could ignite her body as much, if not more so, than the touch of any man.

'So,' she said with an air of finality. 'What now, Tanya?'

Tanya smiled, her wide mouth seeming to almost fill the bottom half of her face.

'You are ready for Hans. He will be pleased.'

Tanya led her from the cabin. 'This way.' She crooked her index finger – as if she needed to.

Mariella attempted small talk as she followed her wide-bottomed acquaintance.

'Where are you from, Tanya?'

'Georgia.'

'Is that where you met Hans?'

'Yes. That is where I met Hans.'

Not much of a conversationalist, Mariella thought to herself, but she persisted.

'What does Hans want me to do?'

Tanya laughed, the sound bouncing like a deep-throated echo within the confines of the yacht.

'He does not want you to do anything,' she stated, her accent adding an odd, cold preciseness to the words. 'He wants to do everything to you – with your permission.'

She laughed again.

They both toppled together as they went out of the door, and Mariella wished she was back on shore, wished she had finished her walk home, wished that Tanya and Hans had not come along. But it was all water under the bridge. All the same, she couldn't help harbouring an element of hostility.

I don't want to go on with this. It seemed an alien thought. After all, Mariella had never been a shrinking violet. Yet she was apprehensive. A sudden roll of the boat caused her to reach out to steady herself.

'The sea's getting rough. Should we really be doing this? Shouldn't we be getting back to shore?'

Tanya assumed a superior look and shook her head in a way meant to be wise, which looked, in fact, a little silly.

'It's like a mill pond. There's nothing to worry about.'

Mariella wasn't so sure, but not being a yachting type, she didn't push the point.

'In here,' Tanya whispered, her voice charged with both excitement and an air of secrecy.

It was the smell that first made Mariella gasp. Hints of sandalwood, spices and a sweeter smell she could not put a name to, seeped like scented steam up into her head and over her face.

Her eyes opened wide and her whole being trembled when she saw the tented ceiling, the darkly draped walls, the hookah, the silk cushions and the yellow canary singing in a gold-barred cage. A Bedouin tent on a luxury yacht?

But the black-clad figure, face half covered, sabre at his side, and tassels hanging from his knee-high boots, was the biggest shock of all.

Mariella's jaw dropped. Her hand flew to her mouth. 'I don't believe it,' she whispered.

Tanya pushed her forward.

'Down on your knees!'

'What?'

A surprised look on her face, Mariella glanced round at her.

'Down on your knees! The sheik commands it.'

Tanya's strong arms pushed her again so she went flying onto a pile of cushions that were conveniently situated at the feet of the black-clad man.

The silk of the cushions enveloped her face. For a moment,

she hid her eyes in them as she fought to come to terms with what was happening to her. This was not her fantasy. Hans van der Loste was acting it out for real.

Her fingers clawed into the cushions. Her thoughts ran in confused circles. Wasn't this the lover she had always had in her mind? Wasn't this the situation she craved? So why did she feel fear instead of excitement?

She gasped as the tip of his boot poked against her throat as he raised her chin. He jerked it so that her head snapped backwards, and her eyes looked up the length of him to his veiled face.

'You are my prisoner. My slave. You will do whatever I want you to do. Do you understand?'

Mariella heard his voice, saw the swinging tassel on his boot. It was definitely the Dutchman. She could see his blue eyes, hear the crackling inefficiency of his accent as he tried to master some sort of Eastern orientation.

The knowledge of who he was did little to arouse her, though his diamonds were going some way to doing that.

The diamond chips were pressing into her belly, digging against her breasts and thighs. It was as though tiny, hard fingers were prodding at her flesh, testing its firmness.

'On your knees!' he ordered.

Once her chin was released, her head fell forward, the diamonds hanging from the skull cap brushing her cheeks and tinkling as they had before. Her breasts heaved as she gasped for breath. She thought hard as she worked her neck in circles to help alleviate the stiffness.

'On your knees!' Hans, the would-be sheik, was sounding impatient. But still Mariella took her time. Defiance had sprung so easily to life, and she had to ask herself why.

Because he's an imposter, said a small voice inside. He's trying to be someone he's not, because Valentino, the real sheik, only lives inside your head. He doesn't even live in Hollywood – he died last year. Anyway Valentino was the sheik only once, his image and passion caught forever in a black and white film watched in a cinema in Vienna. She'd never even heard his voice, only saw his words printed in white on a black background, the organist adding appropriate atmosphere.

No. This would not work. She could not go through with this.

But Hans really was impatient.

Suddenly, Mariella was jerked upright by Tanya's strong hands grasping her shoulders.

'Obey!' Tanya cried, sounding as enthusiastic for whatever part she was playing as Hans was.

So Mariella knelt, the chips of diamonds digging painfully into her knees, her breasts gently rising and falling and still tingling from the pressure of the gems when she had been lying down.

Tanya, the willing slave, stood behind her. Hans – she could not think of him as the sheik – stood before her, his groin directly opposite her eyes. She was aware of his loose-fitting robes swaying. So were the tassels on his boots. But then, why shouldn't they? After all, they were at sea.

A sudden roll of the boat made him spread his legs a little wider in order to steady himself. The first roll was followed by another, and yet another, each one more fierce than the last.

'Tanya! Get up to the bridge and tell that skipper of mine that I'll drop him over the side if he lets this boat roll like that again.' There was urgency in his voice. His gaze did not leave the kneeling woman before him.

'But I . . .' Tanya sounded reluctant to leave her lover alone with another woman.

'Get going!' Hans barked.

Without needing to look round, Mariella knew that Tanya had left them. She fell forward onto her hands as the boat rolled again, fiercely enough to send the canary cage rattling and crashing to the floor.

With the last roll, Hans fell down with her, his body crushing hers and his black robes catching on her dress.

His huge arms clasped her tightly to him.

'You are all mine to do with as I want,' he growled. His lips crushed hers.

Mariella swiftly turned her head. 'No one asked me!' she shouted.

Hands formed into tight fists, she pushed his face away.

He grinned, his arms clasping her tighter before his grin became a mocking laugh.

'That is it, my dear. Struggle. Fight. Hit me and kick me all you like, but you will not escape me. I know you like the playing of parts. The count told me this when he saw this room of mine. He was very surprised that I was so keen on the cinema. He thought it would be amusing. It was easy for us to do a deal.'

'A deal with what?' Mariella still struggled.

'An icon.'

'You're lying! You haven't got the one he's interested in.'

Hans laughed. 'Maybe not. But I did have one that was exceptional. It was owned by the last lover of Catherine the Great. A young cossack officer only nineteen years of age. Her lover when she was almost seventy.' His laugh subsided as a thought struck him. 'How did you know I didn't have his icon?'

Unwilling to answer his question, Mariella began pummelling him about the shoulders. 'Let me go! I don't care about your deal. I don't care about Catherine the Great and her lovers. I am me, and my love life is mine to do with as I please!'

Showers of clenched fists hit his chest, shoulders and face. Still he laughed. Still she struggled in vain, her legs kicking as his hand slid up under her dress, his palm hot upon her thighs, his fingers forceful between them.

'Ahh!' he said at last as his fingers found the shorn nakedness of her pubic lips. 'How soft they feel.'

Despite her anger, Mariella groaned as he squeezed them. With all her might, she willed herself not to become aroused. The effort was unsuccessful. Slow, shivering tingles began to uncurl like the leaves of a new spring flower. She bit her lip to stop herself from purring with delight. Not that Hans seemed either to notice or to care whether she was enjoying his attentions or not.

'How clean, how sweet, how vulnerable. Just as I like them.' Hans sounded in ecstasy. His eyes were half closed, his mouth half open as he savoured the feel of her beneath his probing fingers.

Mariella fought for her breath, and for once, for her honour.

But Hans was not heeding her. His breath was hot against her face. His grip was like iron, and the hand between her legs was tantalising despite her hostility towards him.

'Let me go!'

He laughed at her words.

She kicked him, and he laughed louder.

Just as the first finger found its way into her body, and his lips sucked at her shoulder, Tanya came bursting back into the room, arms outstretched, hands gripping the door surround to stop herself from falling. Creamy skin had turned ashen.

'Hans. I think we have a problem. Dolman says to come right away. We have lost power. We are drifting towards the rocks, and a storm is coming.'

Hans jerked his head back, his face red with rage.

'I will kill that man.'

Mariella caught her breath. 'If you don't do something pretty quick, you won't need to.'

Hans glared at her, red face quickly turning puce. Was he going to strike her for speaking out? For one moment, it looked as though he might do.

'We'll all be dead,' she added, staring directly into his eyes.

As if to confirm what she had said, the boat gave another roll.

Hans rolled off her and struggled to his feet. For a moment, he swayed like a drunken man as he fought to get his balance.

Tanya reached out to help him.

'Hans, do you want . . . ?'

But Hans was not listening. His blue eyes were bulging, his red face pulsating with fear. Desperately, she attempted to cling to his arm, but he shook her off, striking her so hard that she thudded to the floor.

Hans, black robes flying out behind him, charged against the heeling of the floor and lunged for the door.

Mariella stayed on all fours as she felt the floor beneath her fall, rise, tilt one way, then the other. The canary cage rolled across the floor, bars buckling, canary squawking. The cushions rolled after it and the hookah tipped over, spilling its mushy contents over the dark reds and ochres of the carpets.

'We are going to drown!' Tanya screamed as she fell to her knees.

'I will if I keep this on,' muttered Mariella, concentration hard on her face.

Swaying from side to side, she struggled to raise her arms above her head so she could get out of the diamond dress.

Tanya, who was clinging to a length of the dark fabric that had formed the tented ceiling, stared at her as though she were mad.

'Why are you undressing now? He will not be back for you. He must deal with the boat. He must save the boat and save us!'

Mariella barely glanced at her. She had not known Hans van der Loste very long, but long enough to judge that he was a man who looked after his own skin first.

Once the cumbersome weight of the diamond dress was thrown to one side, Mariella crawled on all fours to Tanya whose limbs were now so rigid with fear, they looked rooted in the floor.

'Listen!' Mariella grabbed hold of the big girl's shoulder. 'The way this boat's rolling about, you could be right about us drowning. Do you understand that?'

Tanya's eyes were big as saucers. Her bottom lip trembled.

'Do you understand me?' She shook her again, more roughly this time.

Tanya blinked as though digesting the question. Then she nodded swiftly, abruptly. 'The dress,' she said weakly.

Mariella looked at her in amazement. 'Blow the dress. It's too heavy. If we do have to get into the sea, that dress would most likely drown me!'

Tanya's expression was still relatively blank.

'Wake up, woman! Listen to me,' she shouted as the floor beneath her heeled one way, then another. It plunged forward as they dipped into another slice of mountainous wave, then jerked backwards as another wave followed before they had time to gain an upright position.

'Come on!' Mariella shouted. 'Get your bearings. We have to get out of here, and you know the way better than I do. Is that right?'

Mariella's words seemed to slap into Tanya's face with as much force as the sea was slapping the boat.

'Come on!' She raised her hand and, with as much force as possible, struck Tanya's face. 'Come on!'

Once Tanya had blinked a few times, something seemed to flutter free. It was enough. Mariella knew she was there. The woman's mind was open again. Fear, for the moment, was pushed to one side.

'This way.'

Tanya struggled to her feet. Mariella grabbed her arm, her legs almost crumbling under her as another mighty roll sent the floor slewing at crazy angles. One hand still grasping Tanya, she groped to undo her shoes. The chains were stubborn at first, but she was determined. The shoes were kicked aside and rolled across the floor as if they had a life of their own.

Another small, sign of life caught Mariella's eye.

'Hold onto that.' She placed Tanya's hands against the door surround, then dropping to all fours, she made her way across the sloping floor to where the cushions, hookah, and seemingly everything else was gathering.

Scrabbling among the cushions, she at last found what she was looking for. The canary was still alive, though its cage was slightly dented.

'Come on, bird. We're both flying from here,' she murmured.

When she saw what Mariella had gone back for, Tanya looked at her oddly, but said nothing.

'This way?' Mariella asked.

Tanya nodded.

When they at last gained the companionway that would lead them up to the deck, they heard shouts and thuds from overhead. Squealing winches sounded overhead, and something seemed to be scraping against the side of the boat.

'Are we sinking?' yelled Tanya, throwing her arms around Mariella's neck, almost to the point of strangulation. 'Are we going to drown?'

Mariella fought to disentangle herself from Tanya's arms, then winced as sharp fingernails bit into her upper arm.

'Tanya! Let go. You're hurting me.'

'I don't want to drown!'

Mariella could hear the sound of her own heart thudding against her ribcage. She was as frightened as Tanya, but knew that if she gave way to her fear they were both likely to drown.

'We are *not* going to drown!' And I hope you believe that, she thought grimly to herself, because I'm not sure if I do.

She gripped Tanya's shoulders as she said it. 'We are *not* going to drown!' she repeated. 'Now say it yourself.'

Wide eyed, face ashen, Tanya merely stared right back at her.

Mariella slapped the woman's cheeks again, so hard this time that her red hair swung across her face like a shredded red curtain. '*Say it!*' she screamed as the boat heaved around her, and the canary cowered in its pretty gold cage.

'We . . .' Tanya began.

'*Say it!*'

'We . . . are . . . not . . . going . . . to drown!'

'No!' Mariella shook her head.

'No.'

Tanya shook her head in a weak parody of Mariella's own action.

'Right,' said Mariella, brushing the other woman's hair away from her face as she held her gaze. 'Now we will go up on deck. Right?'

'Right,' Tanya replied.

Only after Mariella had got Tanya moving forward again did she realise the scraping and the squealing had ceased. Surf crashing on deck was the only sound remaining.

Doors swung on their hinges, and crashed against the wheel-house. The power of the wind took her breath away, and the rain splattered her face, stinging her eyes as she tried to focus.

Holding tightly to both Tanya and the canary cage, Mariella chanced one bare foot on deck, then the other. Waves pounded over the side of the boat, beat at their feet, then sucked at them before falling back into the sea.

'Hello!' Mariella cried, eyes narrowed against the surf and the rain.

Through the blinding downpour, she tried to focus on what might be people but turned out to be just flotsam tossed aboard the boat by the heaving sea.

What do I do, Mariella asked herself? Despair made her limbs feel suddenly heavy. She felt drained, not only by the natural forces and the dilemma she faced, but also by the fact that Tanya was clinging to her arm, hair plastered to her head although they had only been outside for a couple of minutes.

'Where's Hans?' she asked, the heaviness of her accent returning to her voice.

Mariella, fear twisting in her stomach like a thick hessian knot, did not answer her. Inside she cursed the man. Women and children first was obviously not the first rule on this particular boat. But there was no point dwelling on it. Survival was all that counted.

She narrowed her eyes, craned her neck, telling herself to look as if there was hope even if there was none.

Out to the east, she thought she could see a number of small lights bobbing about on the sea.

'Lifeboats,' she said quietly to herself, unwilling to let the hysterical Tanya know that their predicament was very serious.

How many lifeboats had been on the *Cartouche*? If her memory served her right, and bearing in mind she had been brought aboard slung upside down over a moron's back, she recollected there might have been two, maybe even three. Hopefully, there were more lifeboat places than there had been crew.

Face streaked by rain, she reached for a coil of rope and lashed it quickly around her waist. Before venturing out, she checked that the other end of the rope was fastened to something secure. It was.

'I'm going to check to see if there are any boats left,' she shouted at Tanya. 'Look after the canary whilst I'm gone.'

Tanya nodded as she took the cage, though judging by her expression, she was none too pleased that Mariella was leaving her.

'I have to do it,' Mariella added.

'Yes.'

It was a small word and said very quietly, barely snatched out of the noise of the storm.

'Hold on to the rope!'

Tanya nodded, seemingly unaware that Mariella had already fastened it to a secure metal railing.

That will give her something to think about, she reasoned, but did not comment.

Salt water lashing against her legs, rain soaking her naked body, she staggered over the deck using any piece of engineering to steady herself.

Without needing to walk the entire length of the boat, she

could see the situation was hopeless. There were no life rafts. They were alone on board the *Cartouche*, their vessel being tossed and thrown by the merciless waves.

Slowly, feeling her way with her hands, and water rippling around her ankles, she made her way back to where Tanya was waiting.

Tanya grabbed hold of her and pulled her inside.

Mariella fell on to all fours. She fought for her breath, spitting sea water out of her mouth and shivering. She stayed like that as she attempted to steady her breathing.

'Are we going to sink?'

Mariella looked at her directly and shrugged. 'Did the life rafts have engines?'

'I think so.'

'So our owner, skipper and crew will not be crashing onto the rocks.'

Tanya, eyes filling up with fear, wrapped her arms around herself and, sobbing, sunk slowly to the floor. 'We're going to drown.'

Her voice drifted into a whimper.

Mariella closed her eyes and shook her head. Why had Tanya turned out like this? Why couldn't she have been a lot braver, a lot more useful than she actually was?

'We mustn't give in.' It sounded obtuse, but it was all Mariella could think of to say before something more profound came into her head.

'Damn you, Peter Stavorsky! Damn you!'

She eased herself back on to her folded legs and leaned her head back against the wall. Only her hair was still dry, the skull cap clinging bravely to her head.

At this moment in time, she hated Peter Stavorsky. And yet it had not always been like that. He was the man who had taken her virginity and had never given her the chance to acquire inhibitions. He was also the man who had reminded her of Valentino, and added life to her daydreams. And where would she be without them?

Not here, she told herself. Not bloody here!

Her head drooped onto her chest. All her strength seemed to have been sucked out of her by the sea, the wind and the rain. Slowly, she sank to her knees. Tanya cuddled close to her. Mariella sensed she was about to say something, but continued to lay her head on her arms, knees folded up beneath them.

'What are you going to do now?'

Tanya's husky tone had disappeared. It was almost childish now; just like a curious little girl.

Mariella brought her head up a little and gazed at her over her folded arms.

She blinked.

'I'm out of ideas. How do you suggest we entertain ourselves?'

There was a crazy look in Tanya's eyes as she considered what Mariella had just said.

'Oh, we could do lots of things. We could teach the canary to talk.'

'We haven't got that much time.'

Tanya looked peeved, but not put out.

'We could play hopscotch.'

She's crazy. Mariella stared at her, pity taking the place of her own despair.

'We're on a boat, Tanya, and its decks are not level enough to play hopscotch. A boat, Tanya!'

'A boat.'

Tanya repeated the word as if the fact she were on a sea-going vessel were a complete surprise to her.

'A boat. Yes. Then how about we let off the rockets?'

Mariella had hidden her eyes in her arms again. At the mention of the word rockets, she slowly raised her head and looked at the steadily crazier Tanya.

'The boat has rockets?'

Tanya nodded.

Hardly daring to hope, Mariella sat upright. 'Do you know where these rockets are kept?'

Tanya nodded again. 'In that locker there.'

She pointed to a locker just below the wheel which was presently spinning madly with each tug of the tide on its rudder.

'Hold on to that canary.'

Again, Mariella was on all fours, fighting her way to the locker.

She almost prayed as the door opened and she saw the batch of distress flares banded in sections stating terms of use and how to activate.

Two, she thought. I'll use two to start with.

Getting the two flares out of the locker was easy. Getting back out onto the deck was more hazardous because this time she failed to secure herself with a thick rope.

But the sea did not seem so rough as it had been.

The first rocket flew up into the air, a shower of red sparks lighting up the sky, then falling like blood-soaked stars.

Before lighting the second rocket, she looked to starboard, almost expecting to see a rescue boat coming out to save them. Between the dips and swells of the waves, she saw the occasional light, but it was far off; probably St Asaph, she thought.

Her hopes and prayers went with her second rocket. It occurred to her then that they should make some effort to rescue themselves. Couldn't one of them steer the boat? Surely it couldn't be that difficult.

Again she scrutinised the sea.

'I'll drive this thing,' she said quietly.

Still she saw lights blinking intermittently on the starboard side.

What she saw on the port side made her spring into action.

'I have to drive this thing!' she exclaimed as a row of what looked like jagged teeth rose above the swell to port.

Shivering now, in need of clothes but still wearing only the diamond-studded skull cap, she dashed back into the wheelhouse.

'How does this work?' she yelled.

Tanya, still sitting in a heap in the corner, was making cooing noises to the canary.

'I do not know such things,' she said slowly, shaking her head from side to side in a thoroughly mournful way.

Mariella swore beneath her breath. It wasn't ladylike, but this was no time for being a lady.

With instant resolve, she gripped the wheel, her eyes studying the dials that told her wind direction, and the points of the compass.

'Due north,' she muttered to herself. 'St Asaph is due north.'

Pushing hard against the swell that still gripped the rudder, she heaved on the wheel until the needle of the compass swung round to due north.

To her great surprise and joy, the boat responded. The wind had lessened, and the sea was calming, though was still nothing like the mill-pond Tanya had described.

I'm doing this right, Mariella told herself as she grappled with the wheel. A gradual change in horizon seemed to occur, even though its clarity was obscured by the rain spattered all over the windows.

'We're going to be all right,' she called to Tanya, a whole ton weight seeming to have been lifted from her body.

Tanya hugged the canary cage to her chest, her face giving no hint that she either heard or cared.

Through the wheelhouse window, Mariella could see a dark shape that appeared each time the waves receded. Someone saw the rockets, she told herself. Well, they're too late now. I'm the skipper on this scurvy ship!

Her bravado was short-lived. Although she had aimed the boat due north, it was still being carried towards the rocks. No matter how often she turned its bows towards St Asaph, it did not seem that was the way in which it was going. The rocks were looming large.

'We're going to have to jump,' she said, panic suddenly replacing her earlier confidence.

She repeated herself but Tanya went on cooing to the canary.

'Get up,' Mariella shouted at her. 'Get up.'

She tugged Tanya to her feet, shaking her in an effort to emphasise the seriousness of their situation.

Somehow or other, she didn't know how, she dragged her companion out on to the deck.

The wind was still fairly strong and caught her breath. Fear drained all softness from her face as she took in the sight of the surf crashing on to the rocks. Water spewed from its crevices, dripped from hanging barnacles each time the waves ebbed away, regrouping like a thundering army to attack the rocks again.

It's hopeless, she thought. Impossible.

Tanya obviously thought the same or felt her own fear. She flung her arms around Mariella's neck, the bird cage bumping painfully against her shoulderblades.

'Let go!' Mariella clawed at Tanya's arms, but the redhead was bigger than her and also stronger. She was also too frightened of drowning to worry about sharp fingernails.

'You're suffocating me!' she shouted before Tanya's arms hugged her even closer to her chest.

A kind of bliss passed over Mariella's body as she smelt the warmth of her companion, her nose and mouth pressed tight against the other woman's breast. She wanted to scream, to fight some more, but what air was left in her lungs was slowly being used up. She was fainting, fading away, smothered by Tanya's mighty breasts.

As she drifted, she saw her sheik. He was sitting on his horse and was smiling. At the same time, he was reaching out for her, beckoning for her to come and join him.

'I thought you had deserted me,' he said, his voice a thick mix of accents she had half heard, half felt in the melting pot of Marseilles.

There was a thudding sound in her ears.

'Are those drums?' she asked him.

He didn't answer. It was as if he were fading completely now, his smile lessening and a sadness coming to his face as he drifted beyond her reach.

The thudding continued, a steady beat that was suddenly interspersed with the sound of men's voices.

The thick pillow that had covered her face was lifted. Had it been a pillow? She could barely remember.

She felt strong arms taking hold of her, gentle voices telling her that everything would be all right.

She heard the canary sing, then heard Tanya telling someone every detail of what had happened to them, and how Mariella had thrown her dress away because it was too heavy and she might have drowned.

Hearing Tanya telling how it was made her suddenly more tired than she had ever been in her life. Her legs collapsed beneath her, her eyes closed as she followed her dream lover into the red-hot heat of her fantasy desert.

'Were you really going to leave me?' he asked her, his dark eyes flashing, his body tight against hers.

She paused before she answered. Should she tell Etienne that he looked even more like Valentino than his half-brother Peter? So much so, that she had found no need to fantasise.

The answer came easily to her. 'How could I leave the man of my dreams?'

Chapter 26

Someone was doing wonderful things to her. Warm hands; gentle, loving hands, were wiping her down with a thick Turkish towel.

Her eyelids fluttered before opening.

Something sparkled to her left. Dark eyes smiled on her right.

'Etienne!'

He kissed her and tasted her amazement. 'You are safe now.'

For a moment, it seemed as though her mind was like a big stock pot, full of bits and pieces all stewing around together. She closed her eyes again and shook her head. It helped clear away the murkiness.

'I was on a boat.'

'I know. Was it you who sent up the distress rockets?'

She nodded. 'Yes.'

'We saw them – Joe and I. Only an arrogant man would have gone out in that weather. Or a very brave one. One of the fishermen brought us out in his boat. It had a big engine. We would never have reached you in Joe's sailing yacht.'

Mariella stared at him before weariness made her close her eyes again. But there were too many questions needing to be answered. She opened them at the same time as she realised she was still naked and Etienne was wiping her dry.

'What happened to Peter?'

An odd sadness came to Etienne's eyes. 'He's gone. With the icon. Joe's mission was successful.'

She bit her lip. She wanted to ask whether he had left any word for her. After all, they had been together a long time.

Etienne seemed to have read her thoughts. He looked away, suddenly embarrassed, then looked back at her again.

'He's not worth worrying about. You had your time with him. There are other times to be thought about now.' He took hold of her hand. 'What do you intend doing?'

Mariella struggled up into a sitting position. Etienne, his palms pleasantly warm on her flesh, helped her.

Unable to meet his eyes, she frowned. 'I need to be free.' The words struggled out.

She looked into Etienne's face and was surprised to see him smiling.

'You don't mind?' she asked.

He shook his head. 'Why should I? Everyone has to be free at some stage in their life.'

She smiled too and touched his face. 'I'm glad you agree, though I don't necessarily think you understand.'

He looked puzzled. He spread the towel over her belly and his hands over her breasts.

'Tell me.'

She was a moment finding the right words. Once she did, she looked him full in the face. 'I want to be free to dream. You might not understand that. I must confess, I don't really understand it myself. You see,' she took a deep breath, 'Hans had the same seed in his imagination; the same dream to some extent. He wanted to be Valentino as he appeared in *The Sheik*. He wanted to fill that part, so he tried to make it reality.'

Etienne was gazing at her still. If he was confused by what she was saying, he wasn't letting on.

Mariella licked her lips and took a deep breath before continuing. 'You see, I need my fantasy as a fantasy. I cannot have the man in reality. If I did, then I would no longer have that man in my dreams and somehow I know I need him, and in a strange way, phantom or not, he needs me.'

Etienne hung his head for a while. When he looked up, his eyes were sad but his lips were smiling. 'Will I see you again?'

She nodded. 'Every time I am in Europe. I can't disregard

you completely. Perhaps when I am completely satiated by my dream lover, I will be with you permanently. But until then, I cannot desert him.'

There was a softness in Etienne's face, resignation in his eyes. 'Then I will wait for you. If you are not in Europe, where will you be?'

She smiled. 'I would like to go to Hollywood. Do you think Joe would take me there?'

Etienne raised his eyebrows. 'You would go with Joe?'

'Of course. He's no threat to my dream lover. I can indulge in my fantasies as much as I like, because Joe is nothing like him and does not arouse me like he does.'

She raised her finger to his mouth and traced his lips with its tip.

'But you do,' she said softly.

He let her sleep after he had kissed her many times, his mouth lingering over the new nakedness of her pubic lips.

As she drifted into sleep, her sheik was there again, sitting on a coal black horse wearing black, flowing robes and reaching out for her.

Sand warm beneath her feet, she ran to him, her body naked, her will utterly subservient to his.

A Message from the Publisher

Headline Liaison is a new concept in erotic fiction: a list of books designed for the reading pleasure of both men and women, to be read alone – or together with your lover. As such, we would be most interested to hear from our readers.

Did you read the book with your partner? Did it fire your imagination? Did it turn you on – or off? Did you like the story, the characters, the setting? What did you think of the cover presentation? In short, what's your opinion? If you care to offer it, please write to:

The Editor
Headline Liaison
338 Euston Road
London NW1 3BH

Or maybe you think you could do better if you wrote an erotic novel yourself. We are always on the look-out for new authors. If you'd like to try your hand at writing a book for possible inclusion in the Liaison list, here are our basic guidelines: We are looking for novels of approximately 80,000 words in which the erotic content should aim to please both men and women and should not describe illegal sexual activity (pedophilia, for example). The novel should contain sympathetic and interesting characters, pace, atmosphere and an intriguing plotline.

If you'd like to have a go, please submit to the Editor a sample of at least 10,000 words, clearly typed on one side of the paper only, together with a short resume of the storyline. Should you wish your material returned to you please include a stamped addressed envelope. If we like it sufficiently, we will offer you a contract for publication.

More Erotic Fiction from Headline Liaison

SEVEN DAYS

Adult Fiction for Lovers

J J Duke

Erica's arms were spread apart and she pulled against the silk bonds – not because she wanted to escape but to savour the experience. As the silk bit into her wrists, a surge of pure pleasure shot through her, so intense that the darkness behind the blindfold turned crimson . . .

Erica is not exactly an innocent abroad. On the other hand, she's never been in New York before.This trip could make or break her career in the fashion business. It could also free her from the inhibitions that prevent her exploring her sensual needs.

She has a week for her work commitments – and a week to take her pleasure in the world's wildest city. Now's her chance to make her most daring dreams come true. She's on a voyage of erotic discovery and she doesn't care if things get a little crazy. After all, it can only last seven days . . .

0 7472 5094 4